PRISONER

NICOLE DERE

CHIMERA

Prisoners of Passion first published in 2000 by
Chimera Publishing Ltd
PO Box 152
Waterlooville
Hants
PO8 9FS

Printed and bound in Great Britain by
Omnia Books Ltd, Glasgow

PRISONERS OF PASSION

Nicole Dere

This novel is fiction – in real life practice safe sex

Chapter One

Splat!

'Oh-ow-yeow!' Feely yelped and swivelled her hips, lifting her bare bottom at the hot bite of the rubber-soled gym slipper that had been brought smartly into contact with it. 'Oh, miss, please! It – it hurts! Please, miss!' Her voice rose sharply, in a squeal that was only partly assumed, for her bum really was throbbing now, and glowing red at the rapid tattoo of stinging slaps which had been delivered. A hint of tears trembled beneath her pleading tones. Miss Liverton – 'Liverlips' to generations of schoolgirls – liked to be reassured that her beatings were more than mere love taps. Well, she needn't worry on that score! Feely thought, as she squirmed in real pain at the crack that heralded the final blow.

But it was almost a feeling of nostalgia that brought a real threat of tears when Feely slowly straightened from the large desk she had been bending over. Gingerly, she massaged the warm curves, the hem of the black gymslip tumbling over her wrists, and falling at the front to hide the little dark patch of pubis, thus restoring her to near decency. The last time Liverlips would ever spank her, Feely reflected, seeing the gleam in the pale blue eyes, magnified by the severe spectacle frames, the rosy tint in the handsome features. And the last time her faithful acolyte, the Deputy Head,

Miss Dyer, would hover at her elbow, ready to lend a restraining hand should the victim prove reluctant or obstreperous.

It was the Deputy who now picked up the dainty white silk panties, with their ruffled edging of fine lace, which had been the official cause of the beating, and handed them back to Feely.

'Rebellious to the last, Felicity,' Miss Liverton chided, but her deep voice was warm with affection. Feely was conscious of their gaze on her as she bent and, stumbling slightly, hauled the delicate garment over the solid black shoes, and the black woollen stockings hanging in ugly folds about her ankles.

'Yes, miss,' she murmured, with a penitent little grimace. She pulled the knickers up, then took the other item Miss Dyer passed over to her. The white elasticated step-ins were dragged up her long limbs, fitted around her middle, then she stooped again and drew up the stockings, smoothing them up her shapely limbs before she clipped them onto the thin ribbons of the suspender straps. She shook out the short skirt of her tunic and it fell into place about her firm thighs.

'You know, your slips are far too short for you gels to wear those disgusting frillies. Why on earth don't you wear your tights?'

'Oh, miss,' Feely protested strongly. The 'tights' were the voluminous navy blue drawers, elasticated both at waist and leg, which were supposed to be worn under the gymslip and stretched down to cover the tops of the gartered stockings. 'The senior girls all hate them. They're so hideous.'

'So you'd rather go round showing off your naked

thighs and those disgusting things you call underwear?'
But Miss Liverton's tone still carried that note of gentle
fondness that belied the throbbing red cheeks now
decently hidden from sight. 'You're eighteen now.
Young ladies. You're not children any more. And
ladies, especially from The Medes, do not go about
displaying their nakedness.'

Don't they? Feely thought wryly, but held her peace.
She knew very well that the Headmistress had sprung
the 'knicker inspection' with the sole purpose of
securing an excuse to smack the delectable bottoms
of Feely and her two bosom chums, before they passed
forever beyond her jurisdiction, and the portals of the
exclusive boarding school of The Medes. The *ménage
à trois*, the staff had jokingly dubbed them almost from
the time all three had joined The Medes five long years
before, for during term times, and a large part of the
hols as well, they had indeed been inseparable.

But even that seemed about to change, in a world
which, over the past weeks, had taken on a
frighteningly unknown aspect in so many ways.
Witness the sudden frantic efforts to move the entire
school away from the familiar Surrey countryside
down to the faraway reaches of North Wales. Adolf
Hitler, at whose antics the girls used to shriek with
laughter during the news reels which were shown in
the gym on Saturday nights, was all at once having a
very serious impact on everyone's existence, including
the trio whose lives had been so pleasantly interwoven
throughout their privileged adolescence. Until a few
months ago they had expected their intimate lifestyle
to continue, in the exciting surroundings of The

Goldborough Academy for Young Ladies, on the shores of Lake Geneva, near Montreux. Now, all that was in abeyance, in spite of her father's desire that the plan should go ahead.

'Be quite safe in a neutral zone,' daddy had declared. Also looming large in his mind, and in those of her chums' folks, was the disturbing thought that young ladies, even of their background, might very well be conscripted in the coming hostilities.

Her friends were waiting for her in the cosily cramped room on the top floor which, as members of the Senior Sixth, they'd had to themselves for the past year. Their faces were flushed, and Feely could tell they had only just sprung apart at the sound of her approaching footsteps. She glanced at the ruffled covers of one of the beds, still clearly indented with the shape of their intertwined bodies, and their hastily donned towels, which were all that concealed their nakedness. 'My God!' she exclaimed, in mock disgust. 'We might be bombed to bits any second but you two still go at it like nymphos at an orgy!'

The girls flung their towels aside and fell back onto the bed, once again wrapped around each other. 'That's precisely why, you idiot,' Possy said. Her angelic face, crowned with its tight-knit cluster of dark gold curls, beamed up at her. 'Come and get your kit off and join us. How's your bum? Rosy cheeked maidens all!' Giggling, they moved in unison, rolling over to kneel and thrust their behinds uplifted in Feely's direction. Each tight little curve had a distinct red patch at its centre.

This arresting sight reminded Feely of how Possy

had come to be given her nickname, that distant day when the trio had first met. The harassed duty mistress was calling from the list of new arrivals. 'B. Hind?' she announced, and looked bewildered at the storm of laughter which greeted the words.

The blonde holder of the name looked almost as puzzled as the teacher at first, then she reddened and her face split in a sheepish grin. 'I've never noticed before,' she confessed. 'My name's Brenda. And I'll kill my folks next time I see them!'

But her name was to be Brenda no longer. Not as long as she was in the company of her two new chums. 'We dub thee Posterior. But as we're going to be such good friends, we'll call you Possy for short.'

The dark-haired one, Felicity Keynes, swiftly became Feely, a vaguely pornographic epithet which she soon resigned herself to, until her proper name almost made her snigger with its unfamiliar pomposity. And the third member of the triumvirate, a figure of ethereal beauty and of delicately elfin features and proportions, of freckled, translucent skin and crowned by a mane of rich, fiery chestnut hair, whose name was Olivia Bowe-Wyndham, acquired the unromantic sobriquet of Olly.

That rich redness was displayed now on another part of her anatomy as Olly turned onto her back once more and carelessly allowed her knees to fall apart. 'Why not come and join us?' she invited, in that slightly breathless, catchy voice that Feely found by turns both irritating and immensely attractive.

'Don't be disgusting!' she answered primly. 'Cover yourselves up! Don't you know there's a war on?' She

9

turned away towards her own bed, and three seconds later was squealing in muffled objection at the two figures who had launched themselves at her with lightning speed and now held her pinned face down across her patterned counterpane. 'Get off me, you wretches! I'm not – oh – I – *oh*!'

Her cries ceased abruptly as, with practised skill, her opponents' hands swept up her stockinged limbs and dragged down, in one glorious tangle, the narrow band of the step-ins and the silk panties. The stocking tops, still attached to the suspender straps, were hauled down with them until the whole mess clung about Feely's knees like bonds and her shoes waved helplessly in the air. In the meanwhile, cool hands were exploring at leisure the still tender curves of her bottom, followed by two pairs of moist lips bestowing tender kisses on the crimson patches.

'Dere dere, diddums. Mumsie kiss it better.'

'Cut it out, chaps,' Feely protested, but her voice had sunk to a sighing whisper, and her objections lacked authenticity. In fact, physically, her resistance had fled, as the naked pair eased down the entangled garments, untied and removed her shoes before slipping the whole lot clear of her stirring feet. Gymslip bunched around her waist, below which she was now as nude as her aggressors, she lay between them, biting at her lip and sighing even more noisily as Olly's delicate hands slid round from their caressing of her backside. The slender fingers played in the tight black tendrils of her pubic hair, before sliding lower to the moist fissure whose fleshy lips seemed to part in dampening welcome. Expertly, a finger-pad delved into the uppermost folds, sought out the tiny beating trigger of desire until soon the entire cleft blossomed, aswamp with the pulses of excitement flowing more and more strongly through it.

'Please,' Feely begged, but whether the plea was for a cessation or for a greater effort towards fulfilment even she no longer knew. Dimly, she was aware of being pulled and rolled back and forth, of the gymslip and tie and blouse, and the vest and brassiere (bosom supporter, in the antiquated language of the school laundry list) being stripped from her. Olly's finger had never ceased the stroking circular motions, squelching away at the centre of her now frantic sexual arousal. When Possy's lips closed over the hard little teat of her right nipple, the excitement exploded into the mindless bliss of climax. She seized Olly's wrist and savagely jerked the hand deeper into her spasming sex, heaving her belly up from the bed in order to impale herself further, her pale body arched and racked with the splendour of the orgasm tearing through her.

She was unaware of the cataract of weeping until long minutes later, and acknowledged her friends' loving with a shamed, sniffling smile. 'God, I'll miss you two,' she groaned, and the three nude figures lay in interlocked harmony until the mellow September light began to fade, and sounds of distant activity made them reach for their dressing gowns.

In the spartan surroundings of the Seniors bathroom, they sat in adjoining tubs of tepid water while they discussed the subject never far from the forefront of their minds – their uncertain future.

'We could always stay on here for another term or

two,' Olly began hesitantly. 'I mean, go down to Wales with the school. Liverlips would be delighted to keep us on. She said so.'

'No,' Feely stated emphatically, and the other two waited for her to go on. She was really the acknowledged instigator and leading thinker of the group. Though athletically the curly-haired Possy was foremost, both she and the easy going Olly looked to Feely for guidance when it came to decisions or new ideas. She was very much aware of this as she spoke now. 'She's smacked my arse for the last time, poor old cow. Time for pastures new, I reckon. For all of us.'

'Daddy said we might still be able to go to Switzerland,' put in Olly tentatively.

'What? Bury ourselves away when all hell is about to break out all around us? I don't think so!' Feely leaned back, lifted one shapely leg out of the water and held it out, studying it critically. Her toes waggled in the steamy chill of the air. 'We're big girls now. I reckon we've had enough of school, don't you? Whatever happens, we're going to get mixed up in this war madness, willy-nilly. They'll be dishing out these call-up papers soon, and even your illustrious pa mightn't be able to pull strings,' she said accusingly, staring across at Olly, whose already pink features deepened a little. Her father, Lord Crossway, had influential fingers in a good many impressive pies.

'Why don't we jump the gun and make sure we all stick together, eh?' Feely continued. 'Let's use our influence in the right direction and get ourselves into the war effort in some outfit where we can all stay united? What do you say, chaps? All agreed?'

'First thing you have to learn in the army is discipline, my girl. Understand?' The thick voice sounded as though its owner was being throttled, an impression fortified by the spectacle of the fleshy, empurpled features, and the bug eyes.

'Yuh – yes, sir!' Olly gasped, twisting round and squinting up through tear-filled eyes and the clouds of her dishevelled red hair, from her position across the corpulent brigadier's knee. Her satin knickers were wrapped around her ankles. Her shoes had long gone, flying off when she began the restrained little kicking movements she knew would rouse the fat old pig even more. It had worked, too, as she could tell from the hard protuberance she could feel thrusting up through their clothing against the pit of her belly. She could feel the drag of her suspenders, the tight band of her step-ins biting into the taut curves of her behind where he had thrust them up to bare her buttocks for the onslaught she was tensed to receive. The silk stockings were still in place, and rasped softly now as she strove to keep her legs together when she kicked out. 'Please don't hurt me, sir,' she bleated, and felt a bitter sense of triumph as she felt that throbbing penis leap at her belly.

Smack! His hand, which had felt so soft and squidgy when she pressed it at their first meeting, was now like a paddle as the open palm slapped at her clenched bottom. The hot glow spread, and was soon overlaid with another as the hand descended once more.

Smack! *Smack*!

She yelped, scissored harder at the throbbing pain. Her silk-shod foot slipped out of a knicker leg. The dainty panties swung from one ankle then flew free, to flutter like a falling leaf to the carpet.

Smack! Smack!

She was wriggling violently now, no longer deliberately trying to intensify his priapic excitement, but reacting to the hot stinging which made her tears stream faster. 'Please stuh – stop!' she sobbed. 'You're hurting me! Oh – oww!'

When at last he did, she slid from his knee to sprawl undignified on the floor, clutching at her scalded bum, rubbing vigorously, unaware of the entrancing spectacle she afforded. She scrambled up, felt the suspenders chafing her hot flesh, could not pull her massaging hands away, though at least her skirt now hid her nakedness at the front.

Let him stare pop-eyed at her legs, the dirty old sod, she mused. As long as that was all he did. Shame stained her upper cheeks almost as hotly as those she was still tenderly stroking as she recalled the sensation of his rising prick pressing against her. Just how much did Feely and Possy expect her to sacrifice for the general good? She'd already surrendered more than enough, she reckoned. She was not going to yield her precious virginity to this decrepit old relic from the War Office, not even for the sake of their carefully contrived plans to fight the war together.

In the event, she was not called upon to do so. Unknown to her, the brigadier's crisis had come, all too stickily abundantly, and it was he now who was the more afraid, when he thought of what Lord

Crossway's youngest daughter might do for his revived career if she should talk of his little weakness. He was ready to grant her anything, within reason, to ensure she would not do so.

A day later, Olly faced her chums in the privacy of the luxurious bedroom of her family's Mayfair apartment. 'We're in!' she told them exultantly. 'We're to join something called the ATS. Army Transport Service. We'll be taught to drive, then we'll be assigned to some Brigade HQ. We could be in France for the spring!' She pouted fetchingly. 'And don't think it was a doddle. Look.' Solemnly she turned her back, bent at the waist and raised her skirt. She flipped down her knickers clear of her behind, and they stared appreciatively at the darkening bruises. 'I thought old Liverlips and the rest at The Medes were kinky enough. Now it seems senior officers are just as bad!'

Feely's dark eyes danced as she advanced towards her. 'Poor little Olly! Kiss better?' she asked, nodding at Possy, who moved with her.

Olly gave a little shimmy and the knickers fluttered to the floor. She stepped out of them. 'Yes, please,' she breathed enthusiastically.

Chapter Two

A glob of thick black engine oil dripped onto Feely's brow, and she stared in hatred at the filthily congealed mess of metal and pipes a few inches above her nose. She longed to reach up and tuck the stray hairs about her grimy face more securely into the tight-fitting cap, but she scarcely had room to wield the big spanner that was locked onto the obstinately unyielding nut of the sump drain. She was lying on her back on a thin wooden trolley under a military truck. She was filthy, her hands coated with grease and oil, her face hardly less so. The baggy overalls were liberally besmirched, and even the old khaki cap was stained. The cold from the concrete floor beat up through the thin layer of wood so that every bone and muscle ached, in spite of the ugly, thick, scratchy flannel underwear. This was the severest winter in years. Several times the water pipes in the camp had been frozen solid, and she thought now with tears stinging in her eyes of the luxurious bathroom at home, the limitless hot water; Sarah, the maid, standing by with fluffy towels fresh from the radiator to envelop her when she rose from a leisurely soak in a miniature snowstorm of fragrant lather.

The ablutions here were even more primitive than at The Medes. Tin baths in a row, to be shared by more than twenty girls. It wasn't the lack of privacy that bothered her; she was used to that after The Medes – in fact, some of the girls from less privileged backgrounds made far more fuss over having to be seen naked by their colleagues. But it was the lack of comfort; the bareness of their surroundings, the scummy grey water you had to leap in and out of, unless lucky enough to catch the first bath.

The unremitting coarseness of their contemporaries was appalling, too. God knows, the ménage were aware of their sexuality, but these working-class girls were so drearily obsessed – and so unoriginal, so crude and limited.

Another blob of oil dripped onto her. 'Fuck,' Feely muttered softly, then felt herself blushing. She was becoming as gross as her fellow Amazons. She had known of the word's existence, of course, but until coming here she would never have dreamt of using it, could not conceive of its ever passing a female's lips.

This wasn't what they had envisaged at all, Feely acknowledged grimly. They had thought in terms of smartly tailored uniforms, officer status. Somehow, it had never occurred to them that they would be expected to endure the unappetising life of the OR's. Other Ranks, as the army termed them. They had visualised themselves sitting behind the wheels of staff cars, whisking officers back and forth, wining and dining with the handsome younger staff officers, dancing at the Ritz and smart clubs up in town, then across in Paris for more of the same. And maybe other, more interesting and private assignations, in comfortable hotel bedrooms. All of the trio were virgins, though technically, Feely sometimes wondered uncomfortably if they still qualified to use the term 'intacta', given the freedom with which they had explored one another's acquiescent bodies. But all three dreamed eagerly of surrendering their maidenhood, under the romantically right circumstances, and partner.

The realities of Wallington Camp were depressingly different. 'Did I let that drooling letch of a brigadier smack my botty for this?' Olly had declaimed tragically that first night in their new abode.

'As long as that's all you let him do,' Feely muttered dryly, and Olly squealed in righteous indignation.

'How dare you? My virtue's still intact—'

'If not your cherry,' Possy cut in, and all three sniggered.

But life was grim and laughs were few, Feely conceded, as she lay beneath the three-ton truck. Far from the apocalypse everyone had imagined, the war was a distant stalemate as they moved into 1940, and the worst enemy was the atrocious weather. It wasn't as if they could seek the private consolations the trio had habitually shared, for their existence was so public. A barrack room full of narrow creaking metal beds, and shared ablutions. Even the lavatories had double half-doors like stable stalls, so that knicker-wrapped ankles were on view and anyone with a mind to could peep over the top and watch you wipe your bum!

Then there was the work itself. Why on earth did they need to learn to march in step, to swing their arms and stick their chests out, and execute all the other endless drills in the mind-numbing cold, in order to drive dishy officers about in smart limousines? And to learn all about the workings of these disgustingly filthy, smelly vehicles and their unfathomable mechanical mysteries, until their fingernails were broken and blackened, and their hands and faces were black as coal and they stank like grease monkeys? It was only pride, the pride of Old Medians, that kept them at it. That, and the fact that if they quit they might well end up in a military prison which would be worse even than Wallington Camp. They prayed fervently each night for the next twelve weeks to pass quickly, and to succeed in the passing-out exams that came at the end of the course.

Feely's gloomy thoughts were interrupted suddenly by a violent tugging at her heavy boots, which were sticking out from the underside of the truck. The suddenness of this event caused her to jerk reflexively, and she smacked her forehead painfully against the metal inches above. 'Hell, Possy! Is that you, you clot? What—'

She tried to slide the trolley and propel herself out from under the vehicle, but another pair of solid boots prevented her from doing so. She squinted down her body to the narrow slot of daylight, saw the gleaming objects which were impeding her progress, and the stiff gaiters with the gleaming brass buckles. They were standing on her insteps, causing her feet to turn outward in a quarter-to-three stance that was grotesquely reminiscent of Charlie Chaplin. 'Sergeant Cameron,' she squeaked indignantly.

The gruff, disembodied northern voice drifted down to her. 'Bloody 'ell, Keynes! 'Aven't you got that sump drained yet, you idle little slut?'

'You've no right to talk to me like that, sergeant,' she answered, but her tone was weak and quavering. More like the lip-quivering little girl she felt like inside when

19

faced with her instructor's blunt, aggressive masculinity. She squirmed, tried to move, felt the strain on her limbs as he easily held her feet trapped beneath his.

'I'll talk to you any fuckin' way I want, slag! I don't know if you realise it, Keynes, you snotty little cow, but you're within an ace of bein' thrown off this course altogether. You're fuckin' hopeless, you know that? And if you get kicked out, you know where you'll go? Not back to mummy and daddy, you stuck up bitch, but to the cookery course at Caterham. Where you'll scrub pots and pans and peel spuds for the rest of this fuckin' war, my girl!' There was a grunt, and his ruddy face appeared in the narrow gap of daylight as he crouched low and peered in at her. Though his feet had moved, she felt his heavy hand pressing firmly on the baggy overalls, just above her right knee.

'Just checking. I thought you 'ad one of your la-di-da lesbian mates under there with you.' He laughed coarsely.

'Would you take your hand off my knee, please, sergeant?' Feely said. She strove to be icily calm, but her voice trembled even more. Instead, the hand slid up her leg, almost to the top of her thigh, and she stiffened in shock. She gave a little gasp.

His voice dropped in volume, thickened in heavy lechery. 'Listen, you stupid cunt. I can make or break you. Haven't you twigged that yet? It's up to me whether you get through the course or not. They all take note of my say-so, even Major Phillips. You play along with me, Keynes, and you're through, no worries. I guarantee it. What do you say, slag?'

Feely gasped again, jerked, and banged her head

again. His hand had slid up to the conflux of her thighs and belly. It cupped the curve of her vulva. She felt its pressure through all the thick layers of clothing. The palm rubbed, pressed against the soft flesh, and to her horror she felt the electric thrill of arousal moistening her labial divide. His fingers were hard, rubbing the length of her narrow fissure, and she shivered, her thighs stirring, closing tight against his invading hand.

'Please, sergeant,' she whispered tearfully, hating herself for her feeble tone, and for the betrayal of her throbbing sex. 'Someone might come.'

The syrupy chuckle was like another of his obscene caresses, and she shuddered at its note of male triumph. The tears trickled down her dirty cheeks to lodge in the wisps of hair at her temples.

'You just lie still, my girl. Don't you worry your pretty little head about that. I've taken care of it.' When she felt his hands at her work-stained boots, she expected to feel herself hauled out from under the lorry, but to her astonishment he left her as she was, with her upper half still hidden under the vehicle. Without hurrying he untied her laces, eased off the great boots, then peeled off the grey service socks.

'Fuck me, how many bloody clothes you got on, then?' He had discovered that, under her army socks, she was wearing a pair of her own long woollen stockings, a relic of more innocent, happier days at The Medes.

He reached in towards her, and she felt his thick fingers fumbling with the buttons of her overalls, opening them up at her midriff. All the strength seemed to be draining from her. She no longer found any voice to protest, but lay limp, snivelling quietly like a child.

21

The fingers had found a way in, now they plucked at the waistband of the khaki serge trousers, negotiated the fastening, parted them at her belly. Remorselessly he plodded on, like a surgeon cutting through the outer layers. The shirt was hauled up, then the flannel vest, out of the sturdy elastic of the knickers, also flannel, the army issue winter bloomers, passion killers as the girls rightly dubbed them.

Except that Sergeant Cameron's passion seemed immortal. Trembling from head to foot now, possessed by a sensation that was strangely, shockingly familiar, which seemed to spread from the damply beating core between her legs, she lay there, unresisting, as the sergeant headed determinedly for that very core, which throbbed evermore damply the nearer he approached his goal. Another gasp, and her warm belly spasmed against the cold touch of a hand on her bare skin. The hand slid down, fingers extended like the groping limbs of a spider, until he was rooting through the small patch of springy curls covering her mound. Teasingly, the fingers plucked at a few tendrils, stretching them, lifting the skin beneath, then the heel of the hand pressed heavily on the little swell of flesh. Involuntarily, she grunted, and her belly lifted in response to the pressure.

The fingers swept on, to the upper folds of the dewy cleft itself, played with the tight fold, parted it, splayed it open to slide into the slippery slopes thus exposed. She drew her knees up, moaned softly, her hips wriggling, entirely controlled by those wicked fingers. 'I – I'm a virgin,' she wept, moving rhythmically to his stimulation. 'I've never—'

'I bet you haven't,' he said roughly. 'You must've

been missin' your lezzy chums then, eh? You're wetter than an Aldershot pisshouse on a Saturday night.'

'Please, sergeant,' she blubbered, squirming violently, her stockinged feet drumming on the damp, chilly floor.

'Please what?' he grunted, his own excitement achingly apparent, bulging out his trousers. His forefinger hooked, slid deeply through into the funnel of her vagina, whose muscles seized upon the intruder ecstatically. 'You're fuckin' tight, I'll give you that,' he breathed.

She hadn't answered his question. He watched her dainty stockinged feet scissoring back and forth, sliding about, her toes curling in the excesses of her passion, and he worked her quickly, his finger plunging in and out of her, feeling the running wetness, the gathering storm of her crisis, his prick bursting with his own tumescence. He flicked his thumb at the top of her vulva, and was rewarded by the wild spasm of her body, her shrill cries as he stirred the tiny nub of her clitoris. She cried out to the deity, her feet did their dance, her knees drummed against the rim of the lorry. She was racked by the force of the orgasm ripping through her, on and on, for an age until, with one last convulsive shudder, she collapsed, sobbing brokenly, her body quivering with the aftershocks of the violent release.

He withdrew his hand, wiped his fingers on her overalls, and she felt the cold on her bare tummy, the wetness at her loins.

'Do yourself up,' he ordered coldly, his words like blows. 'And come to the sergeants' mess at twenty hundred tonight. That's eight o' clock to you, you ignorant slag. Wait outside. You owe me one, don't you,

Keynes? Eh?' He stood, kicked her hard on the side of her thigh.

Her torso was still hidden under the lorry as she hastily fumbled her clothing into place. 'Yuh –yes, sir,' she sobbed.

'Don't worry,' he told her with rough reassurance. 'You do good tonight and you're through with flying colours. You and your toffee-nosed mates. You have my word on that.' He turned to leave, then bent, staring under the truck once more. 'Oh, and for fuck's sake wear a different pair of knicks, eh?'

She did. With a rare sense of noble sacrifice she put on a pair of her daintiest white silk panties, and her finest silk stockings under the ugly army skirt. Sadly, she was conscious of the fact that this would be just about the first sexual episode she would not share with her two chums. Though, one day she would perhaps tell them of the lengths she had gone to serve their common good.

But, in the biting cold dark outside the mess, she felt more like some Piccadilly tart as she waited discreetly for Cameron to appear. He was equally furtive, glancing all round before he led her into the accommodation block and up the stairs, along the bleak corridor to the spartan cell where he slept in solitary splendour.

Except for tonight.

She stood, shivering forlornly, genuinely frightened at this momentous event in her young life. Perhaps he understood something of her feelings, for he was almost gentle as he took her coat, smiled at her. Her brown eyes looked huge, and shone with tears. 'I really *am* a virgin, sarge,' she murmured. A vivid crimson tide swept up her face. 'I've fooled around with my chums. With Hind, and Bowe-Wyndham, I mean. But we – I – I've never done it – you know – had sex, with a boy – a man.'

'Don't worry, love. You'll take to it like a duck to water, believe me. If ever birds were meant for shaggin', you three were.' He reached out, drew down the zipper at her waist, and the thick skirt fell about her feet. Already he was undoing her tie, unbuttoning the khaki shirt and dragging it over her head. He studied her slim form in the matching, lace-trimmed bra and panties, the bare expanse of upper thighs bisected by the slender ribbons of the suspender belt. He hooked a finger in the elastic of the fine knickers and pulled her towards him. 'That's more like it,' he grinned approvingly.

She was oddly comforted when, instead of stripping her naked, he pulled her over his knee, slipped the silk panties off her bottom, and spanked her, playfully, but hard enough to sting, and to cause a pink glow to spread through the clenching rounds. But inevitably, the time came when she lay on his narrow bed, her legs immodestly spread, and stared with fear and a pulsing excitement at the rearing prick, with its gleaming helm, which pointed lance-like at her moist centre. 'Be gentle,' she begged, unable to prevent the tears from spilling over.

And he was.

He knelt between her thighs, let his fingers play in her slippery groove until she was sighing with impatience, allowed his prick to nuzzle almost tentatively into her cleft, before it slid deep inside to claim her virgin territory. It hurt, made her whimper

25

and gasp with pain, but finally, in those frenetic moments when their bellies and their pubic bones clashed together in the last dash to culmination, her moans and grunts were as urgent as his.

Chapter Three

'Well, well! Passed with flying colours, eh? All three of you! And I wonder how the bloody hell you managed that?' The speaker was Madge Allcock, a hefty brunette from the north-east, whose sing-song accent they found hard to understand, but whose antipathy towards them had been apparent from the start. She was a barrack room bully, and most of the girls in the class were wary of her, if not downright scared. The trio had got on reasonably well with the majority of their colleagues, though they had made no real friends. After all, they were a self-contained unit, and besides, their background was so different. The class barrier was difficult to surmount. Feely, Possy, and Olly's speech marked them as 'real toffs'. The other recruits were in awe of them, and even the fearsome Madge's aggression had been somewhat tempered. At least until now. But on this last night, with the results posted and a passing-out party planned over in the NAAFI before the group's dispersal on the morrow, Madge's stored up resentment bubbled over as she saw her last chance of getting at the 'toffee-nosed gits'.

At her accusing words Feely felt the colour flood her cheeks, and hoped that her two companions wouldn't notice her guilt. She felt bad enough as it was, having kept silent about her momentous sacrifice, and even worse about how wickedly delightful the 'ordeal' had been. Now, Madge's broad face was transformed by an ugly sneer.

'Don't tell me you're getting ready for the party? Apart from us, there'll only be men there, you know. I didn't think you three little queers would be interested in cock! Too busy sticking your fingers up each other's quims to be bothered about anything like that!'

Now all three sets of cheeks crimsoned. Feely bristled. 'Would you mind keeping your foul-mouthed accusations to yourself, please?' she said. Her palms itched with a desire to slap that red, grinning face. She was sure no one had any idea of what private little intimacies of affection the ménage indulged in. They had certainly given no hint of such personal things, that was for sure. And it shocked and infuriated her to hear their close and tender relationship referred to in such gross terms. At school there had been plenty of behind the hand sniggering, and innuendo about Sapphic love and so on, as well as grand passions which blossomed and blazed and died. In the hothouse atmosphere of The Medes, there were few girls who had not known at some time the heady joys of adolescent exploration, and gratification. But all with tasteful discretion.

To hear it reduced through the mouth of this harridan to such coarse filth was infuriating. 'And now, if you'll take yourself off, we'll continue getting ready for this evening,' Feely ended cuttingly. She turned away dismissively, but the effect was marred by Madge suddenly shooting out a hand and seizing a fistful of Feely's dark hair, with which she yanked the startled figure round and shook her like a terrier with a rat.

'I say! Cut that out!' Possy commanded, coming at

once to the rescue. Feely might be the spokeswoman of the trio, but Possy was the strong right arm. Built with graceful athleticism, she had distinguished herself on the field and on the courts. It was fitting that she should step in now when violence threatened. She grabbed at Madge's shoulders and grappled with her sturdily.

Unfortunately, the sense of fair play and justice engendered on the playing fields of The Medes, backed up as it was by resolute determination, was no match for the streetwise guile of the back streets of County Durham. In a flash, Madge released the yelping Feely and faced her more worthy opponent. The smile spread in joyful anticipation. Possy continued to hold her firmly by the shoulders and to thrust her away from the crowded bed space where the girls had been laying out their clothes. Madge dropped her arms, only to deliver a short but devastating jab with her right fist into Possy's midriff. Possy folded with an audible gasp as the air rushed from her. She sank to the floor. There was a ripping sound, and Madge stood, waving aloft the woollen checked dressing gown, which was all that Possy had been wearing. A few seconds of stunned silence passed, except for the anguished gurgles and snorts from the naked figure squirming ineffectually on the cold wooden boards. Then, with a series of harsh cries that would have done justice to the crowd storming the Bastille, the other girls closed in.

The trio was smothered, engulfed, by the avenging mob. Their dressing gowns torn from them as detested symbols of their privileged rank, and the three hapless girls shrieked as their naked bodies were borne high in triumph. Their assailants held them up on outstretched arms, their pale limbs waving, their bodies twisting helplessly. They were carried out of the hut, into the cold twilight and across the few yards to the ablutions hut. At first they were too stunned to realise the malevolent planning which had gone into the cruel assault. They were only dimly aware of being stood side by side under the thin metal pipes which held the communal showers, their arms stretched and racked as their wrists were bound painfully with ropes about the shower heads. But, once pinioned, they were fully conscious of the spectacle they presented, their arms raised high, unable to cover any of their nudity, their pert breasts uplifted by their involuntary stance. Possy was still gasping and wheezing, her face beneath the cap of golden curls almost purple. The other two were weeping bitterly.

'Untie us, you beasts!' Feely sobbed, but her pleas only served to increase the merriment of their tormentors.

'They look cold, lasses!' Madge mocked. 'Let's warm 'em up a bit, shall we?' Towels were swiftly soaked in water, then began a cracking fusillade of blows, aimed at first at their buttocks, but as they twisted and turned in their frantic efforts to escape the stinging swats, landed more generally over the whole area of thighs, hips and bellies, until the rosy evidence of this torture could be seen as well as painfully felt. Their capering dance of agony as they hopped about from one leg to the other added to the indignity of their suffering, exposing as it did glimpses of their most intimate flesh, which added to the enjoyment of the girls clustered around them.

It was a good while before the last towel flicked, and the three figures hung there, sobbing desolately. They found, to their dawning horror, that their ordeal was far from over when with a rattling hiss the showers were first turned on, and their sobs turned to gasps as the jets of cold water played over them. But, after only seconds, the water hissed, dribbled, then died away. The audience stared, enraptured.

With an ominous shudder, a second deluge commenced. But this time it flowed turgidly. A sickly, familiar smell assailed their nostrils, and as they opened their horrified mouths in simultaneous howls of disgust and terror, a glutinous black tide of old engine oil engulfed them, spread inexorably down, over their plastered scalps, sealing their features, reducing their screams to choking, spitting dumbness, coating their slim bodies in a revolting film that covered them from head to skittering toes in shining blackness like that of a tar baby.

It must have taken Madge and her cronies hours to fill the overhead tank with the stuff. Jerry can after jerry can, ferried up from the motor stores, for the flow went on and on until the three victims were totally unrecognisable beneath its viscous, gleaming mass, their hair, their features lost beneath its blurring smoothness. Even their pubic hair was reduced to a pointed little black tuft, from which the drips of oil fell to join the spreading carpet in which they stood.

It was a while before they realised they had been left alone. Eyes gummed, nostrils blocked, stomachs heaving with the enveloping stink, they hung there desolately, spitting the glutinous dribbles from their lips. Lips that glowed a vivid, ludicrous red against the blackness. They had no idea how long they remained thus, until one of the duty guard came and found them hanging there, and swore in dumbfounded amazement. He fetched his fellows, and they gathered, staring avidly at the arresting sight, before Feely managed to croak, 'When you've finished goggling, do you think you could do something about getting us down?'

They were too far gone in their misery to worry about male eyes seeing their nudity. Sergeant Cameron himself turned up, and with commendable alacrity and presence of mind, organised a working party to get them cleaned up. They had to stand huddled at the scene of their humiliation while the soldiers hosed them down with stinging jets of cold water, to wash the worst of the filth from them. It took a great deal of water before the paleness of their skin began to show through the coating of black.

The metal tubs were filled with blessedly hot water. 'I think we can manage now, thanks,' Feely told the corporal of the guard wearily, though all five of those detailed to assist them seemed eager to stay and continue giving help. Alone at last, the girls sat and rubbed and scrubbed, shampooed their hair over and over; stood and rubbed at their more intimate parts until the tender flesh stung, and their bodies glowed ruddily.

The party had finished, their tormentors, giggly on weak NAAFI beer and cider, came and stood about for a time, brazening it out but clearly uncomfortable at their complicit guilt. The three figures sitting in the metal bathtubs ignored them, and their former persecutors were soon glad enough to leave them once more alone.

Only Madge showed any belligerence. She stood over them, her face even redder, her speech rougher with drink. 'Mebbe that'll teach you slags not to lord it over the rest of us.' She sniggered lewdly. 'I hope you've cleaned yourselves up properly. Otherwise, when you get home on leave tomorrow and your boyfriend wants to give you a proper shag, his cock'll come out looking like the dipstick on a three tonner!'

'Really, you gels will have to fend for yourselves, darling,' Lady Crossway announced at the breakfast table.

'Of course, mummy. Don't worry about us. We're used to it now.'

Olly's father, hidden behind the *Times*, harrumphed angrily. Clearly the war news, or lack of it, displeased him almost as much as the news on the domestic scene, which was nothing short of disastrous. Olly felt guilty that she herself could not summon up the outrage her parents felt at the way their lives were being disrupted. Pawston Castle, like so many other stately homes and imposing buildings, indeed, like The Medes itself, was being taken over for the duration of the war. Turned into a hospital, or a military establishment of some sort.

'Turned out of our ancestral home like refugees!' Lord Crossway had declared tragically. Not quite, Olly reflected, recalling the newsreels of Polish peasants fleeing from the German advance, with their possessions piled precariously on handcarts. There was still the comfortable town apartment in Knightsbridge, and the seventeenth century house down in Dorset. In any case, with the staff decimated by call-up, or the temptations of much more lucrative war work in factories and the like, there was no way they could continue to live at Pawston. But, dutifully, Olly kept her thoughts to herself, and listened commiseratingly.

However, she was far too buoyed up to share their gloom. The thought of seeing her beloved chums on the morrow, and the excitement that lay ahead for them, made her spirits soar. And she was able to congratulate herself, too, on being largely instrumental in assuring their good fortune by a second visit to Brigadier Dunoon, the elderly roué, and associate of her Uncle Bernard. It was worth the indignity of having his puce, pop-eyed features slavering over her, and of hanging there over his knee while he fondled her, slipped her silk panties down and administered one of his spankings. 'You naughty little minx!' he wheezed, slapping away until she wriggled against his belly and felt once more the throbbing results of her efforts, and his.

Both her upper and nether cheeks were pink at the conclusion, but she had succeeded in fixing things so that the ménage would remain together, in the plum posting to 1st Army Group HQ, sequestered in a chateau only fifteen miles from Paris! Feely and Possy would be absolutely enthralled when she told them, and she derived a great amount of unselfish pleasure at the thought of seeing their joy when they learnt the good news. And they deserved it, too. She shuddered even now when she thought of the nightmare ending of their stay at Wallington.

She strove to push away yet another unpleasant

thought intruding on her happiness. There was another earlier sacrifice she had made on their behalf, one of great moment, about which she had said nothing. It played on her conscience like a nagging tooth, but somehow she could not bring herself to breathe a word to her two bosom companions of what she had allowed to take place one afternoon, in the tiny duty office of the motor stores with Sergeant Cameron, on a creaking camp bed. For the common welfare of the trio, she kept on assuring herself, but it did not make her feel any better. The much anticipated, dreamed of surrender of her virginity – and she could not impart this shattering event to her two closest chums. And shattering was the word! Painful it had been, physically, but not as painful as the image stamped on her mind which relentlessly returned again and again – of her bare feet lifted towards the girders of that unimposing edifice, peddling away while her thighs dug into that solid, pumping flesh cleaving to her, and she shrieked with the lost enthusiasm of a devotee of the hunt riding towards the savage triumph of a death.

The remembrance caught her again, and she shivered, felt that electric quiver through her loins and belly, which caused the colour to rise once more, despite the earliness of the hour.

The thoughts of mounting, of sturdy beasts between the thighs, drew her steps almost helplessly through the deserted kitchen garden towards the stables. It was odd that she should think of the hunt. She had never been very keen on field sports, and she was content with a sedate jog on the faithful mare, Kitty – and even that would not have happened all that frequently had it not

35

been for Harry Turner.

The stable lad was there, as she had known he would be. The horses would soon be sent away, too. Harry expected his papers any day now, was looking forward to it. He was only a few months older than she was. They had grown up together, he had taught her to ride. And one or two other things, she recalled, smiling at their adolescent smuttiness. But over the last year or two things had become different, their relationship had changed. He had grown surly, uncommunicative, and she felt awkward in his presence. Last summer, towards the end of the holidays, when everyone was waiting and hoping against hope there would not be a war, she had come upon him quietly one evening. He was standing just inside one of the stables, washing at a standpipe before going off duty. He was stripped to the waist, his shirt hanging from his unbuckled trousers, and she stared at his slim, hairless body. His beautiful body, she realised, breathless at the knowledge, feeling as though her insides were being churned to water. The unmistakable ache centred squarely between her thighs, caught her unawares with its force. She could feel her mons swell against the cotton knickers, felt the pressing dampness over that secret cleft, and almost fled.

'What you gawping at?' He had heard her, turned, towelling his arms and neck, and she blushed vividly. 'How'd you like it if I sneaked up and watched you having a wash?'

She gasped at his insolence, his belligerence, but could not find her voice to reprimand him. She had seen him, of course, lots of times since then; he had accompanied her out riding as before. But the knowledge of that meeting was there between them. She had the shameful feeling that somehow he had known the sensations racing through her mind, and her body.

Now, with her imminent departure and his, the sense of their whole way of life coming to an end, she felt compelled to go to him. 'I'm glad I've caught you,' she said resolutely, glancing around the yard, seeing that they were alone.

'At least you haven't caught me with my pants down,' he answered, and she felt her face flushing hotly.

'I didn't that other time,' she said, her voice unsteady.

'No. You had a damned good try, though, eh? What you want then?' His question was rough, carried that truculent tone which denied the difference in their status.

She swallowed, suddenly discovered that all such things, which she had taken for granted, were uncertain, hardly mattered any more. She shrugged, the blood darkening her pallid skin, hiding the dusting of freckles about her nose and cheeks. 'I thought... with my chums coming tomorrow. Then we're off back in three days... I might not get the chance... I wanted to say goodbye. Properly. To let you know – I'll miss you, Harry.'

'Miss me?' He laughed, the violence startling her. Her heart was thudding, her legs felt weak. He nodded at the jodhpurs, her shining, calf-hugging boots. 'Come for one last ride, have you?' Another ugly laugh, and she blinked at him, shook her head faintly. 'Well, that's what you can have!' he snarled and, seizing her by her arm, pulled her forcefully into the shadow of the stable building, pushed her brutally into the nearest empty stall. Her violet eyes were huge, like some helplessly trapped animal as she stood, legs apart, staring at him.

'You know how I've always felt about you – *Miss* Olivia!' he ground out, making her name sound like an insult. 'Oh yes, you've known! Got a great kick out of it, I fancy, eh? The filthy peasant leching after his lordship's girl. And I have! Lain awake many a night, a hard-on like a bone, tossing myself off while I tried to imagine the impossible!'

She had a sudden urge to hysterical laughter. He believed he was shocking her. Maybe even thought she wouldn't know what on earth he was going on about. Well, she'd grown up in the last three months, and heard far worse from her gallant contemporaries. A sudden vivid image of Sergeant Cameron, his solid body, that great red-headed prick bobbing at his loins, came to mind, and she wanted to laugh aloud again. Instead, she drew a sobbing breath, gave him her most soulful, little girl look. 'Harry, I swear, I had no idea. What is it you want? Tell me.'

'I'll fucking show you!' Now his cry sounded like a sob as he launched himself at her, dragged her down into the thick layer of straw. She felt him scrabbling, tearing at the waist fastening of her breeches, tugging them down. His fingers clawed at the cotton knickers under her flapping shirt, hauled them down too, until jodhpurs and knickers clung in an imprisoning band about the tops of her riding boots. She was turned over, pinned down over his raised knees as he sat in the straw. My God, not again! she thought abstractedly. She might as well be back at The Medes! Why was everyone so determined to thrash her bottom? Surely he would see the fading bruising from the brigadier's chastisement only a few short days before?

If he did he gave no sign, and they were soon hidden under the hot and ruddy glow he caused to spread over her clenching, dimpling nates. He spanked hard and fast, and her booted feet scuffed and jerked in the straw until her sobbing cries for mercy were all too genuine. 'Please! Stuh – stop. I'll do anything…'

He rolled her over on her back, fought off the tight boots, then the tangled breeches and underwear, leaving her clad somewhat inelegantly in the thick woollen socks. He knelt, fumbled, and she saw advancing towards her a slimmer but equally rampant prick, and she knew as she parted her legs to receive it that here was a second secret she would keep from her chums.

Chapter Four

'Well! I must say you chaps are a distinct improvement on the drivers we've had round here so far, eh, Captain Young?' Lt Col Burden's plump, pinkly pomaded face split in an ear to ear grin of delighted lechery.

The three girls smiled in dimpled appreciation and breathed a little deeper, thrusting out their modest but pert bosoms for his further delectation. They knew they looked good. The expensive alterations they'd had done to the design of the ATS uniform, the individual fittings, and the remaking in a much finer material than the coarse serge of the originals before they had left for France, had proved well worth the effort. The hem of the skirt now rested well above their knees, a good four inches shorter than the standard regulation length, which ensured a generous view of their shapely legs, encased in gossamer silk rather than the lisle stockings issued to them. There was nothing they could do about the solid, flat-heeled service shoes. They would have loved to replace them with the high heels they looked so good in, but they knew that would have been pushing their luck too far. Besides, their sartorial changes had already achieved the desired effect, to judge from the drooling expression on Lt Col Burden's ruddy features.

But a growling rumble in the back of a throat warned them that not everyone held the same view. Captain Clarissa Young's face was also highly coloured, but not, the girls sensed, with approval. Lt Col Burden, RASC, was undoubtedly their commanding officer, in charge of all the transport for 1st Army Group, but Captain Young was the senior WRAC officer, and as such, held a much more immediate control over their existence. As they swiftly found out, after their dismissal from Col Burden's office.

'Come with me,' Captain Young said brusquely.

As they followed her down the corridor, dusty motes dancing in the sunbeams pouring through the long windows which looked out on an orderly scene of sloping, well mown lawns and regimented shrubbery, the girls studied the athletically broad shoulders and solid backside.

Standing at least five ten in her shining shoes, Clarissa was impressively handsome, in a Wagnerian way, and could drive a golf ball further than many of her male colleagues. The three newcomers grimaced mischievously behind her back, but they were full of *joie de vivre* at all that had happened to them since they had entrained at Victoria the previous day.

'What do you reckon, chaps?' Possy murmured, her blue eyes sparkling. Her golden curls jerked back in the direction of the office they had just left. 'He looks like a jolly old bum pincher, at least. Maybe even a spanker. What do you reckon?'

They snorted delicately with suppressed laughter.

Captain Young paused before a door. 'In here.' She nodded, held the door open for them, and stood aside to let them pass.

'Thank you, ma'am,' Feely smiled demurely, smothering the urge to giggle at what she still found an absurd mode of address.

But their smiles quickly faded when, the door securely shut, Captain Young leaned against it and barked, 'Line up there! In front of the desk and stand to attention, dammit! You're not bloody mannequins at a fashion parade!'

They stood, backs rigid, buttocks clenched, arms stiffly at their sides. 'Although that's just about what you look like,' continued the captain, with a loud sniff of disgust. 'Certainly not like serving soldiers, that's for sure. The only serving you look fit for is the kind offered by the tarts round Piccadilly. And I bet you're equally disgusting underneath, aren't you? Eh?'

The frightened faces stared straight ahead, not daring to move as she wandered around behind them. Then Olly gave a startled gasp.

'Keep still!' Clarissa roared, and they flinched. With her officer's cane she slowly lifted Olly's skirt. The trembling girl felt it press against the back of her silk clad limbs, felt the material tauten and strain at her waist as the captain exerted more strength to force the skirt higher. The tan stocking tops, and the suspender clips fastened to them, came into view.

The slender cane was bending under the strain, and Captain Young withdrew it. She moved round to their front, went behind her desk and sat. 'Lift your skirts!' she ordered, with a thin, malevolent smile. 'Let's continue with the fashion show. Come on!'

The scarlet faced girls gawped at her in dismay, then, as the smile was replaced by a frown, gingerly they held the garments and slowly began to raise their hems. 'Come on, for God's sake. I said a fashion show, not a peep show. Higher!' she snarled, gesturing with impatience, and soon the skirts were bunched around narrow hips, and there, on full display, were the stockinged limbs, above them the white thighs, bisected by the even whiter ribbons of suspenders, and above that, the daintily frilled satin panties so favoured by all three.

'Well, well,' Clarissa breathed, the smile again appearing on her florid face. The brown eyes lingered over the entrancing view. 'A whores' convention, no less. What on earth did you sluts think you were coming here to do? No, no, keep still. Don't lower your skirts. Not yet. I need time to take this in. To realise just how far you high class tarts will go in your depravity.'

They stood there, faces burning, tears threatening, their skirts hiked about their hips. There was a lengthy, ominous silence. 'Not exactly King's Regulations, is it?' Captain Young asked. By contrast, her voice sounded reflective, almost friendly. 'Goodness knows what punishment this will merit when the CO's informed. Days in jankers, I suspect. Though I should think you'll be on your way back to Blighty this time tomorrow. Such a pity!'

'Oh please, miss – I mean, ma'am,' Feely begged. Her eyes filled with tears, they sparkled on her dark lashes. 'We're sorry! We didn't know – I mean – we'll do anything…' Her voice faded. Now all three noticed the sudden change of expression that came over the features of the woman facing them. A heightening of colour, a movement of the narrowing eyes, swiftly calculating.

'I don't see how I can prevent it coming out,' she

mused, as though thinking aloud. 'Unless, of course, you're prepared to accept any punishment I choose to give. Then we can let the matter rest right here, in this office.'

'Oh yes, please, ma'am! Anything! Whatever you say! We swear, it'll never happen again, ma'am!' The tears spilled over. They already had more than an inkling of the way matters were progressing. It was like being back at school. Their bottoms were already clenching in anticipation as they stumbled out their fervent thanks. Nor were they wrong.

'Very well, bend over... there!' The thickened voice, the slight quiver of excitement, was enough to betray her, in spite of the effort at calm, authoritative detachment. 'I intend this to be a painful lesson for you. One you won't forget. Lift your skirts at the back. Let me see those disgusting frilly knickers again.' Side by side, hips rubbing, the girls leaned over, their breasts resting on the surface of the desk, and raised the skirts up off their behinds. They were not surprised when the rasping voice went on. 'Now, slip your pants down. Come on, right off your backsides. I want to see bare bums, you little harlots. That's what you're going to get. A jolly good thrashing on your bare arses, and thank your lucky stars I'm being so lenient. And you can just unhook those suspenders at the back there. I don't want anything at all coming between you and my little tickler here. Now, keep still. And I'd advise you to keep quiet, too, unless you want half the staff bursting in to see what's going on. Tuck your shirttails in your mouths if you have to. Right!'

They took her advice, stuffing the cloth into their

mouths. They lay, heads turned sideways, bodies tensed with genuine fear. They knew this would be no token spanking, no sharp little tap with the cane. This was the grown up world, and this sadistic bitch was about to lay it on thick. Their buttocks, palely proffered, dimpled exquisitely as the firm rounds tightened, waiting for the first blow. But they were still shocked when it came.

Feely, on the right, was the first.

Splat!

The slender swagger stick whistled softly the instant before it struck, bit in a deep, flaring red line of agony across the cleft, neatly bisecting it. Feely yelped, jerked upright in spite of her best efforts not to move, clawed at the rippling fire, a loud sob shaking her.

'Down!' Clarissa hissed, and weeping uncontrollably, Feely obeyed.

Splat!

The cane lashed at Olly's delicate little nates, with the same agonising effect. The redhead was in the middle, pressed upon from both sides, but still she jerked free, clutching at her scalding bum, sobbing wildly.

'Oh, oww! No – please—'

'Down!' The command was inexorable, and weeping bitterly, Olly, too, lowered herself once more across the desk.

Somehow, Possy managed to stay sprawled over the desk, though her body jerked, the gold curls sprang upward before dipping again, and a whimpering cry came through the muffling wet cloth she bit down on.

The soft whistles of the descending cane came swiftly then, one after another, followed by the sharp reports as it bit into the quivering rounds, marking them with vivid parallel bars of suffering. The hips writhed, bodies jerked, the muffled squeals, the heaving sobs, came thick and fast. The silk clad legs rasped softly at the involuntary movements, the shuffling little dance steps of agony that sent the clinging, ruffled bands of the knickers to slide and fall until they hung about the slim ankles.

'Mu-mmmph!' they blubbered into the self-imposed gags. Tears splashed almost as hotly on their upper cheeks as the thin red lashes marring their lower. It seemed an endless ordeal but, eventually, they realised from the steadiness of the burning skin, that the thrashing had ceased.

Clarissa Young stood behind them, breathing heavily, and moistly aware from the tight crotch of her own plain service issue knickers, of how satisfying chastising these cute little bitches had been.

'No,' she chided softly, when one of them showed signs at last of stirring. 'As you were. Just lie there, my little sluts, and savour what it means to break army regulations around here. Even for you blue-blooded examples of degenerate aristocracy. Don't worry, I know your sort. Too high and mighty to follow rules like the rest of us. Can't understand why you aren't ruling the roost in here the way you do in that privileged outside world of yours. Well, in here, chickabiddies, things are mighty different.'

She was toying absently as she spoke. Feely gasped, and her stinging cheeks tightened once more as she felt the metal-tipped edge of the slim cane inserted in the deep divide. It pressed invasively, and for a shocking instant, it pressed against the hidden tiny pucker of her

46

anus, which in turn clenched in instinctive revulsion. But the grazing tip slid on, and Feely shivered at the smooth touch of the bamboo, gliding now along the narrow groove until it nudged at the nestled base of the vulva, seeking out that even slimmer groove, the lips fringed by the tiny hairs that adorned it. Feely gasped again, and her teeth nibbled at her lip even while those nether ones tingled at the novel invader sliding serpent smooth between them. There was a subtle pressure upwards, as Clarissa moved her wrist with the delicate skill of an expert fly fisher, and now Feely's thigh muscles locked, and a shiver of response pulsed through her. The cane moved, sawed lightly back and forth like a violin bow, and indeed, Feely trembled, rather like the string of the instrument that would respond so sensitively to such a movement.

Clarissa noted all of it, the tremors, the clenching backside, the sudden locking of those exquisite thighs from which the stockings drooped forlornly. Her own hidden loins thrummed in sympathy. With reluctance, she slid the end of the cane free, visualised the fragrant film of moisture which would be all but invisible on its surface, like sweet breath on a mirror. Sternly, she conquered the almost irresistible urge to bring the swagger stick up to her nostrils and breathe its heady perfume.

'Right, cover yourselves. And let that be a suitable lesson for you. Remember, you're my girls now, and if ever I catch so much as a whiff of fraternisation with all these hole-hungry men surrounding us here, I'll make you choke on those silver spoons you were born with. Right?'

'Yes, ma'am,' they chorused dutifully, wincing as they eased the slippery satin over their fiery bums.

Feely tapped nervously on the door. She felt another sickening bout of envy as she thought of Possy and Olly, ferrying their bevies of junior officers in the staff cars off towards the combined headquarters in the distant capital for the all day conferences.

She'd had only one day of it herself – a delightful day, which had included lunch at a riverside café with two charming lieutenants, even though each time she moved, in the car or out, she had an aching reminder of Captain Young's lesson on proper behaviour. And now, this morning, had come the summons to attend her. Hence the churning tummy, the sudden desire to run to the lavatory yet again.

'Come in.' Feely drew a deep, unsteady breath, and entered.

The room was tucked away on the top floor of the chateau, in the east wing; a small, spartan cell identical to a myriad of others which, in the good – or bad, depending where in the social scale you were placed – old days, the hordes of staff required to run such a huge place had been quartered. There was a single iron bed, a dressing table and chest of drawers, a small desk and chair, and, by the tiny curtained window, an uncomfortable looking armchair and a small round table to keep it company. In one corner stood an old fashioned washstand, complete with basin and ewer, and towel hanging over the rail. This then was the dragon's lair, where the monster lived.

'I've decided it'll do you good to serve as my batman

48

for a while; bring you down a much-needed peg or two. All three of you can do it, on a rota basis. You, lucky girl, have been chosen to be first.' She chuckled grimly. 'I don't suppose you've any idea how to look after somebody, have you? Probably can't even look after yourself properly. Too used to having someone do it for you. Wipe your pretty little backside for you.' She chuckled. 'And speaking of backsides, how is it, by the way? Still sore, I hope.'

She ignored Feely's polite mutter of reply. 'First things first.' She clicked her fingers, gestured brusquely, and when Feely gazed blankly at her, said irritably, 'Knickers, man. Let's have a look.'

Feely needed no second bidding. There was no hesitation as she lifted her skirt to her waist, to show the drab khaki knickers, with their elasticated legs, which adorned her loins. Beneath the short gap of pale thigh, were the rolled tops of the thick lisle stockings, held up by the broad service garters.

Clarissa chuckled, nodded again, and Feely let her skirt fall. 'Good-oh. Don't worry, Keynes, I still think you're gorgeous.' She came over and, with playful force, slapped Feely's bottom, hard enough to make her wince. 'Whoops! Sorry. Still tender, are we? Never mind.' She turned, bent in the corner and drew out a pile of clothing. 'While we're on the subject of smalls – first job. Wash these for me. I hate sending them to the laundry. Christ knows what those perverted sods over there would do.'

Feely gathered up the articles, saw that they were a collection of undies, not all army issue.

'The bathroom's at the end of the corridor. Nice hot water. Give 'em a good scrub, my little scrubber. And

49

rinse 'em well, eh? I don't want to be hawking indelicately at my crutch at mess dinner, do I? That done, you can report back here at twelve hundred. Start on cleaning the place up.'

As Feely turned to go, her arms full of the dirty clothes, Clarissa stopped her. A large hand came up, cupped around the delicate line of Feely's jaw, and stayed there, warm, caressing. The deep eyes held Feely's stare. She felt like a mouse before a hungry cat, and just as helpless. 'You know, you might find we can get along very well, after all,' the captain murmured, her mouth so close that Feely could feel her warm breath on her face. 'Especially if you're a good little slave and do exactly what I tell you. Right?' The eyes held her again, with a look so nakedly explicit that Feely felt herself blushing from her shoes upwards. 'Run along,' Clarissa laughed throatily, and sent her on her way with another swat on her shapely behind as she passed through the door.

Chapter Five

'You look a little hot, my dear. Maybe you're a bit overdressed. Seems a shame to have you sweating up your uniform, or getting it grubby. Let's see if we can make you a bit comfier, eh?' The deep voice grew hoarser, and Feely held her breath. Captain Young came up close, and Feely steeled herself not to move away, or flinch. She had been expecting just such an approach at any time during the past two days.

Clarissa had just returned from the bathroom. She was wearing her thick grey dressing gown. Her short brown hair was damp and darkened from the shower. Flecks of iron grey showed in it. The almost rugged face was pink, smelt freshly of the rather masculine but pleasant soap she used.

'She's a dike, no doubt of it,' Feely had told the other two the previous evening. 'I'm warning you, I'll jolly well clock her one if she tries anything on with me.' But now, as Clarissa raised her hands with that mad grin of hers which sent a shiver down Feely's spine, the hapless girl stood motionless, trembling, once more overwhelmed by that sensation of helplessness.

'Things are going to get a lot more exciting round here any minute now,' Clarissa crooned, her face hanging over Feely's shoulder.

You can say that again, Feely thought wildly, the urge to giggle bubbling up again. But she knew Clarissa was referring to the war situation. The whole place was in a flap. The Norwegian campaign had gone disastrously, rumour had it that we were planning to evacuate our troops, that any day now the Germans would move against our defences on mainland Europe.

But Feely had other more private and immediate concerns. She had been summoned to clean up the captain's room. She could feel the amused gaze of Clarissa fixed on her as she inexpertly commenced her task, was even more embarrassed when her superior casually began to strip off her clothes. She tried not to look, but Clarissa said, 'Pass me my dressing gown, will you, Keynes?' She was wearing khaki vest and knickers. What else? Feely thought distractedly, and they showed the solidity of her body, its unfeminine bulk and hardness. She had removed her stockings. Feely could see the ugly red indentations where the garters had gripped the meaty thighs, and was deeply relieved when Clarissa departed for the washroom. Now, though, Feely was all too aware that matters had reached crisis point.

Thick fingers began plucking at Feely's shirt, undoing the buttons, exposing the light ribbed cotton vest, with the dainty strip of lace at the plunging V of her bosom, and the shoelace-slim shoulder straps. 'I'm sorry, ma'am,' Feely stammered, scarlet faced. 'But those army issue vests are so hot. Now that the weather's changed...'

Clarissa clicked her teeth and shook her head in good-natured reproach. 'Oh, you little tart. You just can't forget about sex, can you? I expect you're missing your boyfriend, eh? Have you got someone special back home? Or are you too busy enjoying the efforts of my fellow officers to get into your panties to worry about him?' She had drawn the shirt off Feely's shoulders, and her hands had switched to the waistband of the skirt, which was soon dealt with, and fell in a heavy pool at Feely's feet. 'Well, well! Wonders will never cease!'

The captain faked surprise at the sight of the pale cotton knickers – much lighter and less substantial than the winter woollies, but still mundanely functional and far from the ideal as an undergarment in Feely's eyes. They were, however, regulation summer issue.

Obeying the nod, Feely stepped out of the skirt and stifled a gasp as the captain crouched and, with unsteadily clumsy hands, eased down the black garters, then peeled the grey stockings off Feely's legs. 'Lift up,' she said, as though talking to a child, and Feely obeyed once more, reaching hesitantly to hold on to the bent shoulder, raising one foot then the other while the captain stripped off the stockings.

'There, that's better, eh?' Clarissa laughed gruffly, settled back on the bed, carelessly exposing one leg as she did so. 'Get on with it, girl.' Her voice was still jocular.

Feely restarted the task of dusting, acutely conscious now of her state of undress and, even more, of the captain's eyes following her every move.

All at once she stopped, turned to her, her brown eyes huge, shining with tears, her voice quavering with appeal. 'I… I'm embarrassed,' she said breathlessly. 'Please… don't watch me.'

'You're not telling me what to do, are you, Private

Keynes?' The deep voice was full of mockery.

The tears spilled over. Feely sniffled abjectly. 'Nuh – no, muh – ma'am. I'm sorry.' Head down, she shook as the crying fit increased its strength.

The bed creaked. Suddenly Feely was aware of the tall figure, the arms encircling her trembling frame. A weakening wave of sobbing engulfed her and, with a sweet sense of surrender she gave way to it, leaned in to those sturdy arms, that warm bulk, laid her head against the grey woollen bosom. The hands stroked her dark head, the back of her slender neck, her bare, heaving shoulders. A finger crooked under her chin, pulled up her head, and Feely saw the plain face shimmering through her tears as it swooped down on her. The lips sought hers almost savagely, pressed against her so that she felt the teeth behind them, opened her own mouth, gasping, to allow the invasive tongue to thrust into her.

The world spun dizzily. Feely wondered if she were swooning as she felt herself scooped up in those incredibly strong arms and carried over to the narrow bed. She was dumped unceremoniously on the counterpane.

'You wicked little minx,' Clarissa moaned in a strangled voice. 'You know damned well how sexy you are, slut.' She was crouching, kneeling by the side of the bed. Her sweating face was pressed avidly against the coolness of Feely's thigh. She wriggled violently, fought off the thick dressing gown, then came up in an animal-like spring to plaster her whole naked body along the length of Feely's slender frame.

Feely was startled, in the midst of her confusion, at

54

the size of the breasts that flopped softly against her own slighter orbs, still concealed beneath the cotton vest. Dressed, Captain Young had appeared to have little if any bust. Now the white rounds pressed dough-like against her, the centres marked by generous areolae, crowned with deep reddish-brown nipples of rubbery erectness. They were many times larger than Feely's own more pointed teats. And it was these that Clarissa was now energetically attempting to bare. The large moist hand forced its way up inside the material of the vest, straining it, pushing it over the midriff until the object was achieved, and Feely's pale breasts popped into view. At once the hot face dipped, that consuming mouth opened wide, searching, rooting, closing over the delicate pale pink of the budding centres, and sucked hungrily.

The slim body underneath arched and Feely gave a long, wavering cry, which sank to a deep groan. She shuddered, assailed by the deeply rousing sensation tingling through her. She yelped in a sudden stab of pain as Clarissa, carried away by her own irresistible tide of passion, fastened her teeth around one of the tiny dugs and nipped hard.

'Oh, you glorious bitch,' Clarissa moaned, and buried her face in the fragrance of the bared and palpitating belly. Her tongue sought thirstily for the delightful little eye scoop of the navel, showing in the gap between the rucked vest and the elastic of the knickers.

'Mine, you bitch,' the hoarse tones growled, and Feely shook and wept, and was helpless to prevent the hands which gripped her panties and, with an amorously violent tug, revealed the curl-capped treasures that lay beneath. Feely's hips twisted, but offered no threat to the removal of her knickers, as Clarissa swiftly drew them off her legs and feet and tossed them aside. The creamy shoulders were raised and the last garment, no more than a ruff around her neck now, was pulled over her head. She lay back, as naked as the engulfing form that spread deliriously over hers and strove to make thrilling contact along every inch.

'No, no…' Feely whimpered meaninglessly, lost in the throes of an excitement that swept her along in a cataract of bodily hunger. Urgent hands pulled at her, spread her legs wide, and she drew up her knees, offering herself, lifting her belly to the assault, crying out ecstatically at the touch of the consuming mouth, the lapping tongue, the gnawing teeth, in the flowing centre of her need. Only seconds after two rigid fingers ploughed their way through the tight but yielding tissue of her labia, to enter and claim the spasming sheath of her vagina, Feely's belly rose in one last convulsive heave, and the coming tore through her with the overwhelming power of a tidal wave. A wave that washed from that spasming centre, to every twitching nerve, as far as the tips of her curling toes and outstretched hands. She rode on those buried, conquering fingers, the sealing mouth, entirely at their mercy, lost in the physical bliss no thought could contain.

A lifetime of experience had passed when, a minute later, she collapsed, lay shivering and inert, sobbing in the now smothering but gentle embrace of the pale body over hers, and tasted the unique flavour of her own love juices on the lips that possessed her with a lover's right.

Feely was deeply embarrassed by the affectionate, proprietorial air adapted towards her by Captain Young, particularly in the presence of the other girls in the unit. Her two chums knew at once, without Feely having to supply the graphic details, that bounds had been overstepped.

'She's had you, hasn't she?' Possy demanded. The question was purely rhetorical. In any case, Feely's tearful blush was an eloquent answer.

She was startled herself at the defensiveness which made her snap back untypically, 'Well, what about you two? Given up your cherries yet? What about that Lt Postlethwaite?'

'I wish!' Olly sighed, so fervently that Feely could not help but smile, and the abrasive moment passed.

However, having conquered, the captain's amorous inclinations roamed wider. There was one other rendezvous of loving, prefaced by Feely being stretched over ample thighs, knickers at half-mast, to endure a spanking delivered with open palm. It was no more than a prelude to their love play, though boisterous enough to raise a ruddy glow on Feely's bottom, before feelings of greater intensity replaced the stinging nates.

Next day, Feely was brusquely informed by her lover that she was no longer required to act as personal servant, and that Olly was to assume batman duties with immediate effect.

Feely clicked her heels in exemplary fashion. 'Yes, ma'am.' She professed to heartfelt feelings of relief when she passed on the message to her apprehensive chum, but was ashamed to discover in a painful bout of self-exploration that her emotions at her abrupt dismissal were, in truth, far more ambivalent. 'My best advice is to lie back and enjoy it,' she told the anxious redhead, somewhat unfeelingly.

But, two days later, she was her sunny self once more, despite the growing mood of uncertainty and 'flap' on the official scene. All the girls were kept busy, working far longer than regulation hours as they ferried the staff officers up and down the unfamiliar French roads to various sectors of what would be, all too soon it appeared, the Front.

Gordon Postlethwaite was dishy. That was the universal opinion of all the girls in the driving pool, and so there were sighs and colourful oaths of envy when Feely had the luck to draw the fabled name. The flappiness at HQ had increased tenfold with the news that the German forces had invaded the Low Countries. However, a different campaign was being outlined in the early May sunshine.

'He got his hand up above my knee when I took him over to Francourt. I'm sure, if we'd had more time... one more trip...' Possy's bosom heaved at the depth of her regretful sigh, then she shook her golden head. She tried to stifle the ignoble but overpowering envy she felt at Feely's good fortune.

Feely grinned and winked. 'I was worried in case Clarissa turned up for one of her lightning inspections. But don't worry.' She patted the khaki gas mask container. 'Silk stockings, satin knicks, and step-ins. All safely tucked away in here. I'll find time to change somewhere, I'm sure.'

She did, and was glad. Gordon Postlethwaite was everything she had imagined, and more. Lean and handsome, tightly waved, fragrantly pomaded black hair, immaculately trimmed thin line of moustache contouring his upper lip.

'So you're another Old Median?' he crooned, on the way through the busy roads towards the capital, and the French regional intelligence offices at Surennes. He leaned forward from the rear of the car, so close that Feely felt his breath stir the back of her neck and send goosebumps chasing each other delightfully up and down her entire body. 'Seems to be an absolute rash of you girls over here.'

'I'm not *that* old, sir,' Feely dimpled. Her brown eyes caught and held his in the mirror.

'But old enough, eh?' His fingers toyed with the stray curls below her cap, brushed the nape of her neck and she shivered anew.

'Careful, sir. We don't want a prang, do we?'

Six hours later, the car was parked in a field close by, carefully screened from the road. Feely and the lieutenant were stretched out on a rug, and beside them lay a picnic hamper. The bottle of white wine was almost empty, the sandwiches eaten.

'I've played hooky,' Gordon confessed, when he emerged much earlier than expected from the offices in the village outside Paris. 'No one knows what the devil's going on anyway. I think we can take some time off from this silly war.'

Now he reached out and began to play with her foot. The toes, with their varnished nails, showed mistily through the silk as they curled and twisted at the tickling touch of his fingers. She had slipped off her shoes, rolled up her sleeves almost to her shoulders, removed her tie and opened her shirt as far as decorousness would allow. Maybe just a little further, for the shoulder straps of her brassiere peeped out, and the valley between her pert breasts.

'These aren't regulation,' he admonished, pinching the silk material covering her big toe.

'Oh, don't you start. You sound like old Clarry. She's always inspecting us, making us show...' she stopped, blushing prettily. 'Checking to see if we're – properly dressed,' she ended breathlessly.

'Maybe I should carry out a check myself – just to make sure. I'm a very conscientious officer.'

His cupped palm rested on her slender ankle, then slid up to the swell of her calf, on to her knee, displacing the skirt a little as he did so.

'Yes, I've heard,' she breathed, watching his face coming closer. 'And I'm not. Properly dressed, I mean.'

He bent over her and she lay back on the tartan rug. His lips brushed hers. 'You're absolutely right.'

She gasped as his hand drove suddenly up, under the skirt, clutching at the fullness of her thigh. His fingers plucked at the suspender strap, moved on to the coolness of her bare skin, then toyed with the lace edging of her panties. By the time the searching fingers had moved on, over the pouting swell of the dampening silk covering her mons, and explored the groove of her vulva, his lips had descended, sealed her cries, and her mouth opened, as eagerly devouring as his.

He stroked her, she felt her increasing wetness, squeezed his hand hard between her thighs. 'I'm – I've never gone all the way,' she panted when they finally broke the kiss.

'We could all be blown to smithereens this time tomorrow,' he grunted, never ceasing to work at her. 'Things aren't normal. Think what you might miss.'

'Is that an order, sir?' She tried to smile, felt the tears spring to her eyes, then she wanted only for him to go on touching her, rubbing down there, where all was wet with her fierce desire. Then she wanted more, felt almost as though some other force had taken over her will and her body. Her hands fumbled at the bulge at his crotch, plucked and fought with the infuriatingly reluctant buttons until, savagely, he thrust her fingers aside, released himself, and there, at last, she felt, for the second time in her life that throbbing male appendage made for her narrow sheath convulsing so hungrily to receive it.

Chapter Six

'Can I go now, ma'am?' Olly's face was beet red as she finished adjusting the gartered stocking top and let her skirt fall into place.

Clarissa smiled, amused by the thought that the petite redhead's blush matched almost exactly the shade of that cute little derriere she had just tucked back into the cotton panties after the captain had given it a vigorous drubbing by way of a fond farewell.

'Give my best to Lord Crossway next time you write home, young Windybowes.' It had given her a great deal of pleasure to reflect that she was pleasuring the daughter of a peer of the realm during the week that Olly had served as her personal slave. It had thrilled her nearly as much as the sexual delights they had shared to watch the slim chit of a girl performing the umpteen menial chores she had put her through. 'Tell him I've been keeping his little chestnut filly in line, won't you?'

Olly nodded, and gave her throbbing backside an extra little massage, just for effect. She knew how much this randy old she-goat appreciated such a spectacle. 'Yes, ma'am,' she murmured meekly, her head lowered. It was essential she played her part in keeping the silly old dike happy, in order not to impede the exciting life the three girls were experiencing in the course of their other duties.

Nevertheless, Olly was glad that Clarry covered up

that gross nudity with her dressing gown before she slipped an arm round her shoulders and escorted Olly to the door. 'That's it. Your stint done – for now. Tell Blondie to report here at, oh, seven hundred tomorrow. And don't forget to tell her, two sugars in my morning tea, there's a good girl.'

'I say, you're on next, Possy, old chum,' Olly informed her friend minutes later. She was stripping off, eager to get under the showers, and displayed her reddened bum before pulling on her robe. 'I'll warn you now, she's in spanking good form.'

Possy shrugged stoically, trying to ignore the tiny quiver of excitement at the base of her belly. Both Feely and Olly had made it clear that the duties involved in being Clarry's batman went far above and beyond the call of normal duty. Or was it below? She sniggered smuttily to herself. It would be yet another novel experience in the tapestry of life that was becoming more and more intricately woven with each passing day.

In the heady sexual diversions she and her chums had shared throughout their long association, Possy had generally preferred the more active role. True, she had allowed them to reciprocate the sexual manoeuvres she had bestowed upon them, and with equally shattering results – in fact, it was the intensity of those orgasmic experiences that made her think that on the whole she preferred to be the giver rather than the receiver of such devastating wonders. The loss of control was awesome. Almost too good, in a scary kind of way. On the other hand, exercising that degree of control, holding such power over her victim lovers was in itself a powerful aphrodisiac.

She was in no doubt, though, that with Clarry at the helm, her own role would be entirely passive. She was both apprehensive, and shamefully roused at the prospect.

A further incentive to embrace her fate was her secret guilt towards her two bosom buddies. For the second time in their life together, she was hiding from them events of vast moment. The first had been Sergeant Cameron's northern cock. The mighty engine that had truly sundered her virginity, about which she had remained shamefully silent. True, the sacrifice had been made for all three of them. Time and time again, she had sworn she would confess. Unselfishness had driven her to such extremes, they of all people would understand. Why then had she never made her admission? Was it perhaps the fact that it had been so divine, so wickedly delightful, that rutting animal shag, so perversely different from the sweet intimacies of feminine loving they had henceforth shared? After all, how could she confess that, on that squeaky iron bedstead in that hideous little room, she had screamed and wept and kicked her feet at the ceiling, and come and come until her eyeballs were popping?

At least with Gordon Postlethwaite she had been sworn to secrecy. 'Promise me, you won't breathe a word – not even to your chums,' he had urged. 'They'd be devastated. They think…' he had blushed modestly, '…well, they rather think I'm quite keen on them.' Then he had taken her in his arms, the smouldering look in those splendid eyes melting her as always. That, and his busy fingers, which had found their way through the elastic of her knickers and were working with such cumulative success on her narrow fissure, which was opening in response to his efforts. 'Whereas, you know darned well, Brenda, my angel, that you're the only one I'm crazy about.' Seconds later, those dampened knickers lay discarded on the floor in the back of the car, along with stockings and step-ins, and she was straddling him, her skirt hauled up about her waist and his splendidly erect prick driven hard into the tight hole so recently vacated by his fingers.

Yes, indeed. Her conscience troubled her badly, particularly as far as Feely was concerned. She had seen the poor girl packing her silk panties and stockings hopefully in her knapsack, known how fervently her sweet comrade in arms had dreamt of knowing the utter bliss which Possy herself had come so magically to know.

She had even tried, obliquely, spurred on by her guilt, to ease the poor dear's pain a little. 'I shouldn't worry too much about Lt Postlethwaite,' she advised casually one day. 'There's plenty more fish in that sea, eh?' Her heart ached with compassion at the bravely enigmatic smile, and the pink dusting of the pretty cheeks as Feely acknowledged her words of comfort.

So it was in a mood of noble atonement that, at seven the next morning, she tapped nervously on Clarry's door, the cup of tea trembling slightly in her other hand.

Three hours later, shortly after the captain's return to her quarters for her mid-morning break, Possy stood before her clad only in her vest, massaging the resilient rounds which had received a brief but stinging flurry of slaps as she hung over Clarry's substantial thighs.

Those thighs were parted, and Clarry drew the hesitant figure between them. She took over the job Possy had been doing, and rubbed at the warm buttocks affectionately, staring at the sandy fleece which was on offer only several inches from her nose. Her pink tongue poked out, licked her shining lips, savoured in anticipation the taste and textures of those other lips, so excitingly within striking distance now.

'That little spanking was just to ensure you'll be a good little slave, Hind.' She chuckled. 'You've got the right name for it, anyhow.'

Possy shivered. She could feel the warm breath stirring her pubes, stared down at the grey flecked head so close to her belly. 'Yes, ma'am,' she whispered, thrilled to the core at her unaccustomed subservience.

Her compassionate twinges of remorse towards Feely might well have been eased considerably had she known that, at that precise moment, her chum was in an even more comprehensive state of undress, lying back, on top of the covers in the upper room of an out of the way estaminet several miles distant. Her knees were drawn up, legs crossed, one dainty foot swinging, while she waited for Gordon Postlethwaite to join her.

He was finding it hard to get on with the task of stripping off his own clothing, distracted by the spectacle spread before him.

Feely had crossed her hands behind her head, and her breasts, their pink tips sharp with arousal, attracted his gaze. He stood there, his arms still caught in his shirt, his underpants prominently bulged by the straining penis they contained.

Following his gaze, Feely squinted down at her own

bust and frowned critically. 'I've not got much on top, have I? Do you wish I was bigger? Like Betty Squires?' Betty was one of the other drivers, a full-chested brunette whose rolling backside under her khaki skirt always reminded Feely of her favourite childhood pony, Bobble.

Gordon thrust aside the memory of those magnificently ripe orbs hanging with warm ripeness in his palms. It had been long weeks before. He pulled a face of gallant disagreement, shook his dark tousled head. 'Bollocks!' he declared passionately. This little filly liked a bit of rugged coarseness, both in language and action.

'Yes please, sir.' Feely snickered, gazing pointedly at the protuberance stretching his underpants. Seconds later she was squealing in thrilled alarm as a naked Gordon knelt and rolled her over onto her tummy. He captured her wrists, bent them together up into the hollow of her back. Her pink heels beat rapidly in the air and she drummed her feet on the counterpane. 'Beast, sir!' she gasped, quivering with excitement, and conjured fear. She felt him pinning her wrists, then binding them tightly together, the bonds cutting into her and trapping her effectively. He had used one of her stockings, and she pouted in protest. 'Hey, careful with those. I'm down to my last half dozen pairs.'

'Oh, you poor, destitute little thing!' Laughing masterfully, he let his fingers trail over the entrancing rounds of her bottom, savouring the rippling movement as they clenched and hollowed at his touch. His fingertips traced the deep divide, and enhanced her wriggling motion.

'Don't,' she gasped, her tone an unsteady plea, both of them squeezing the utmost pleasure from their roles. 'Don't hurt me.'

His palms were stroking firmly, fingers strongly pinching the flesh, then playing over the backs of her thighs, the muscles bunching at his rousing touches. 'This bum of yours looks remarkably unsullied,' he mocked. 'Captain Clarry's not been paying you much attention lately. Looks like it's up to me to make sure you toe the line.'

Feely giggled. 'She's got other fish to fry now. Poor Possy's her latest catch. She starts her tour of duty as personal slave today.' Although neither was aware of the other's feelings, each experienced a sharp stab of conscience at the mention of Possy's name, and for reasons, had they but known it, that were not unconnected. Feely because she felt bad about deceiving her friend; the sin of omission, though at least she had the excuse that Gordon had asked her not to say anything about their relationship.

'I'm afraid your Possy has got rather a thing for me,' he confessed ruefully. 'I don't think it would do her ego much good if she found out I'd fallen overboard for you.'

'Well, you just make sure you're nice to her when you see her,' Feely had said, ashamed of the little thrill of pride his words had roused. 'But not as nice as you are to me,' she added roguishly.

The amorous lieutenant sternly banished the vision of Possy's lithe body. His palm descended, delivered a ringing slap on the firm curves below, and the slim figure writhed, the limbs threshed, the feet see-sawed divinely.

'Ouch!' Feely yelped. 'You brute! That hurt! Oh-ow! No, please!' Her voice rose sharply, the rat-tat-tat of blows quickened until the cheeks were covered at their centre by a satisfyingly ruddy flush. The stinging brought genuine tears to Feely's eyes. She felt the cool cotton of the coverlet rubbing against her tummy and thighs, felt the hard points of her nipples brushing against the material.

She began to fight, struggling against the bonds that held her wrists in the middle of her back. The silk burned her sensitive skin at her attempts to escape.

She squeezed her thighs together, thrust her belly forward into the yielding softness of the mattress, feeling the moistening spasms spreading from her vulva through her captive frame. Her voice sank to a catchy whisper, the urge to cry suddenly quite real. Her helplessness added to her sexual arousal. 'Don't hurt me, please,' she begged. 'Be gentle.'

He turned her over onto her back, so that she could feel her trapped knuckles pressing up between her shoulder blades. 'Untie me. Please.'

He was kneeling astride her, his knees either side of her thighs. His prick reared, erect, purple at the exposed helm, which gleamed with his juice. It seemed to tower over her, and her vagina convulsed wetly in anticipation.

'Please,' she whispered again, and he laughed, a resonant chuckle of triumph, for they both knew just what she was begging for.

He tortured her until the tears fell trickling from her eyes, and her belly lifted imploringly towards the majesty of his cock. She felt his fingers at the outermost edges of her vulva, peeling back the tissue, opening her like some unfurling, gleaming flower, revealing the shining darker surfaces of her sex. His thumbs held her open, and slowly he lowered himself, allowed only the tip of his throbbing prick to rest against the glistening divide, to slide feather-light along the groove, and she whimpered, her belly straining to make closer contact. 'Patience,' he breathed, gently moving his hips back and forth, still letting only the lightest contact to be made, until she began to sob.

'Do it, please…' she implored. 'Put it in me.' Her narrow hips jerked, flung up to meet that nuzzling prick. His own urgency could not be denied any longer, and at last Feely shuddered with fulfilment as the throbbing column slid deeply home into her sheath.

She had expected the world to explode, as it had whenever such union was achieved, but not with the shattering roar which erupted now. A roaring thunder which filled her head seemed to fill her body too, shaking it like a dog with a bone, then an ear-splitting crack that shook the bed itself. The world darkened, the roar dimmed then came loud again, drilling into her skull, and all at once, at the very instant when she had felt the mind-numbing ecstasy of his entrance, came the nightmare plucking of his prick and his body from her.

He had gone – gone from her entirely. Left her wide, gaping, empty, lost in a whirl of confusion. A confusion in which weird sensations impinged on her reeling consciousness – the still trembling room, the untoward darkness, and a powerful stench of something burning, acrid. It was some time before her rocking senses identified it as gunpowder.

There were screams, shattering glass, more roars, and more detonations. Bombs? She felt as though she must wake any second from this dream, realised belatedly that this was harsh reality, as she raised her head, opened her eyes to a room full of billowing smoke, Gordon's receding figure, already out of the door as he was still hauling on his clothes.

Attack! *Germans*!

The words rang crazily about her head as she screamed his name, made to leap up from the bed and fell back. Oh God, no!

'Gordon!' She shrieked his name again, fighting furiously to free her hands from the bonds, swinging her legs, wriggling until she stumbled off the bed, staggered and ran across to the open door.

She was halfway down the stairs. A sea of white faces stared up at her – the proprietress and another female face; a red-cheeked girl, one of the servants no doubt, her mouth gaping. Behind them a couple of men, one with a grey drooping walrus moustache, the other younger, all burning eyes, open mouth.

Gordon came into sight, collarless shirt still flapping open. 'For Christ's sake, Felicity!'

All at once she was aware of her nakedness, made to hide herself, cross her arms over her breasts, plunge her hands to shield her dark capped belly. She felt the silk stocking bite deep into her twisting wrists and she screamed shrilly, turned, and fled back up the stairs.

'You stupid bloody idiot!' Gordon yelled, his eyes bugging, his face chalk-white. 'It's an air raid. We're being attacked! Get some bloody clothes on!'

'How?' she screeched, turning her back to display

her tethered hands.

'Fuck me!' he exploded. His fingers tore frantically at the knots, fumbling, taking an age to loosen them.

Her own hands felt useless as she tried to fumble her way back into the clothes scattered carelessly about the room.

Gordon had gone, left her alone, and she sobbed bitterly as she finished dressing, ran back down the stairs. Outside the scene was one of mayhem. A column of dark smoke arose from a neighbouring building. An army van was parked next to their staff car, and a British corporal came up to her, grinning. She recognised him from the base. He winked at her. 'Sorry to spoil your fun, love, but Jerry's on the move. Looks like we've been caught with our pants down. If you'll pardon the expression.'

Chapter Seven

The chateau was swarming with frantically dashing figures, bumping one another in the corridors, colliding in doorways. A carpet of discarded papers lay like snow underfoot. Several oil drum incinerators were burning on the lawns, sending thick clouds of black smoke into the cloudless May air. The short turf was churned with endless criss-crossed tyre tracks. It looked as if every vehicle 1st Group possessed was parked haphazardly on the grass and the gravel driveway. The ATS girls were standing in a tight knot, anxiously awaiting orders in this panic evacuation.

Captain Young, her shining face even ruddier than normal, beckoned Possy and Olly over. 'Well, that little cow of yours has really dropped herself in it now.'

Olly gave her most soulful look. She was convinced that, of the three of them, she was the one Clarry most favoured. 'Why, what's wrong, ma'am?' she asked respectfully.

'Come off it, don't bat those great big Miss Innocent eyes at me. You both know where she is, don't you?' At the simultaneous denials, she gave a cynical hiss. 'No good trying to cover for the slag now. She's been caught off in some knocking-shop with Gordon Postlethwaite. The gorgeous lieutenant who can't keep his dick in his trousers. Or out of that slack-arsed chum of yours! What is it you call her? Feely, is it? Well, she's felt plenty of him all right! Apparently at it like dogs on heat somewhere up near Surennes when the place was strafed. The CO's been trying to locate them ever since we got the orders to pull out.' She laughed grimly. 'Well, tough shit! We're moving as of now. We're heading for La Fourchette.'

The two girls stared at her in horror. Their minds were racing on the same track, trying to cope with the riotous emotions stirred up by the captain's news. Without knowing it, their thoughts were almost identical. Feely! How could she?

Gordon! How could he?

Yet, somehow, their age old loyalty to their chum, battered as it was by her wicked infidelity, came out on top.

'But ma'am,' Possy protested. 'What about Fuh – Private Keynes? What's going to happen to her? Can't we go and find her?'

'No you bloody well can't!' Clarry exploded. 'Let Big Prick Postlethwaite take care of her! They can share the same cell while they're waiting for their court martial!'

'Listen,' Possy said fiercely, when the girls were alone a few minutes later. 'We can't leave Feely – the bitch.'

Olly's eyes widened at the heartfelt epithet, then her heart gave a sickening lurch of shocked dismay. Why on earth was Possy so steamed up at her? Unless… oh no! Olly's face darkened. She felt the rush of threatening tears, a choking lump that she could not swallow. Oh no, not after all they'd done, and he'd said. Sworn her to secrecy – 'Please don't tell the others. They won't understand, how I feel about you.' She heard his earnest words, felt again his gentle hands moving under her skirt, sliding up between the narrow edging of her panties, finding the moist core of her melting need for him, undressing her with such tender, sure love. Riding with her in that steaming, stabbing frenzy on the wide back seat of the staff car, her stockinged heels banging against the door panel, beating a tattoo of lost ecstasy… She stared solemnly at Possy, her violet eyes swimming with tears.

'What can we do?' she whispered helplessly.

'Go back and look for her.'

'But she'll be… she's with…' she had to swallow again, force the words out, '…Lt Postlethwaite. He'll take care of her.'

'Prick Postlethwaite!' Possy exclaimed, her young face twisted with venom. 'I want a word with him, too!'

Olly took a shuddering breath. 'Me too!'

Possy stared at her, watched the colour flooding the delicate features. 'Oh no, not you as well?' The expression of compounded misery and guilt answered her question. 'Looks like we've all three been well and truly shafted. And I mean *shafted*!'

They dashed off to find Lt Col Burden, who was surrounded by a mass of lesser henchmen. Possy gabbled out her request, and he frowned distractedly. 'For God's sake. Jerry planes could be overhead at any second. It's your pal's own silly fault.'

'Oh, please sir,' Possy sighed intently, standing very close and putting her hand on his arm. Her blue eyes gazed up imploringly.

'Oh, for Christ's sake. Take the little Standard. Try and make it to La Fourchette as soon as you can. By oh eight hundred tomorrow at the latest.' He snatched at a pad and scribbled his signature on an order sheet. 'Give that to the motor pool. It's my authorisation. And be careful.'

'Oh, thank you, sir.'

Col Burden's eyes widened. For a second he thought they were going to kiss him, despite the public nature of their surroundings.

Soon, their kitbags stowed in the back, they were heading north east in the little Standard 8, in its drab military colours. They were battling against an increasing flow of vehicles of all descriptions, military and civilian, all making in the opposite direction. Possy sat tensely at the wheel, her knuckles white. 'This is hopeless,' Olly whinged, staring at the chaos all around them. 'They could be anywhere. They'll have started to make their way back towards the west.'

Possy shook her fair head. 'I don't know. All of a sudden I'm disinclined to trust that slimebag Postlethwaite. Would you?'

But, hours later, when the sun was almost sinking behind the trees on the horizon, and they had pulled off the narrow road to give the car a chance to cool off, she was almost as pessimistic as her companion. They had managed to find the estaminet, endured the behind-the-hand sniggers of the owner's family, and followed the indicated path of departure. Hope had been briefly ignited when a local farmer asserted to having seen the dark-haired girl and the handsome English officer, and had led them along this quieter country road, but without any success.

'It'll be dark soon, Possy,' Olly murmured nervously,

looking around at the darkening fields, the shadowy hedges and tall trees. 'We seem to have wandered off the beaten track. We ought to think about finding our own way back. We've given it a good go.'

Possy sighed shook her head. 'I don't know. I just don't feel right about things. Can't explain. It's – holy shit!' She squealed in fright at the startling apparition of a figure which had materialised out of nowhere at the window beside them. Olly's scream echoed her own.

A face bent close, a sunken, unshaven visage, dark locks of hair falling greasily over his forehead. His grin displayed broken, yellow teeth, with numerous gaps. His collarless shirt, originally white, was a ragged shade of variegated grey, the dark jacket and trousers equally grubby, with pale rents where the lining showed through. But his most arresting feature, as far as the terrified girls were concerned, was the giant shotgun whose double barrels were pointing so menacingly in at them.

'*Viens-y*... Out!' The gesture was unmistakable, and the girls scrambled to obey.

'He thinks we're Jerries,' Possy gasped, and then gestured at their uniforms. 'Non, non. *Anglais*. We are English. soldiers. We look for our *ami*... friend.'

He smiled back, but the grin gave them no comfort. He nodded enthusiastically and waved the gun even more threateningly. 'Yes, yes. English friend... come.' He growled at their hesitation, thrust the barrel of his weapon at them, and Olly gave a tiny whimper.

'We'd better do as he says, Possy. He'll blow our heads off otherwise.'

Still gripped by fear, the girls clasped their hands on their heads and began to stumble over the sloping field towards the line of slender trees. The twilight was rapidly fading, and the low block of buildings seemed to loom out of the gathering darkness. There was a large, dilapidated looking farmhouse, and a series of ramshackle outbuildings clustered around the muddy, stinking yard at its side. It was to the largest of these, a double storey barn that reeked of mouldy hay, that he led them.

In the gaping shadow of its wide doorway the man paused, held the shotgun in the crook of an elbow while he unhooked a lantern, fiddling with the wick to light it. 'Please, we are English soldiers. You must let us go,' Possy said, her voice cracking.

Olly was sniffling quietly, already fearing the worst. For answer, the peasant merely gestured roughly towards a wide wooden ladder that led up to the loft.

'Oh God, Possy, what's he going to do to us?' Olly moaned.

Possy nodded at the ladder. 'Just do as he says,' she urged. 'We can't argue with that gun.'

Falteringly, they climbed. Possy was too distraught to think of the enticing spectacle she presented to the upturned face below, though the toothy grin showed that the stranger appreciated the vista of shapely stockinged limb and misty hint of bare thigh, suspender strap and lacy underwear on offer.

The girls stood in the thick straw, blinking about them, until the figure came up and held the lantern high. The circle of light fell on a pale figure, sitting in the dirty straw. A figure whose slim naked body was stained with a liberal coating of dust and grime. The ankles were tethered by a rope, another bound the wrists tightly together, while a third was passed like a halter around the slender neck and bound her closely to the solid upright post against which she was propped.

Their eyes met and the triple shrill cries rang out simultaneously. 'Feely!'

'Olly! Possy!'

But the joy of their reunion was cut short by the peasant's angry interruption. He let fly a stream of French, accompanied by explicit gestures with the gun. Feely's voice came out as a sandpapery croak. She had always been the star pupil at languages, but both Olly and Possy had caught the gist of his demands. 'He wants you to take off your clothes,' she said. 'Do as he says; he's absolutely bonkers.'

Reluctantly at first, but speeding up at the frantic movements of those pointing twin barrels, the girls stripped.

They dropped their skirts onto the straw, then the ties and khaki shirts. His anger appeared to ebb a little as he observed them in cotton brassieres and lightweight summer panties, and the dark stockings, even though they were the standard service issue and, in the girls' private opinion not at all becoming. Their unsteady fingers unclipped the suspenders, pushed the thick stockings down to ankles, then they stooped and removed shoes and stockings. Almost synchronised, they unhooked the narrow little girdles of their step-ins and dropped them on top of their discarded clothing. Elbows winged, they reached behind, fumbling a little awkwardly to negotiate the catch of the brassieres, then, with identical little stooping motions of the shoulders, slipped them off their breasts.

A pink tongue flickered out, licked the liver-coloured lips in acknowledgement of this pleasing sight, and in anticipation of the greater pleasure to come.

Thumbs hooked in the elastic, then thrust down the panties to bear their last secret beauty, their dainty mounds, crowned with two contrasting triangles, one a light sandy blonde, the other a rich chestnut. There was a slight rustle, then twin hiccuping sobs as the girls bent, stepped out of the knickers and deposited them on the top of the two little piles.

'*Tres bien*!' The leering visage bobbed up and down enthusiastically. 'Very good! *Asseyez-vous. Vite*!' They didn't need Feely to translate. Gingerly, they lowered themselves, feeling the sharp ends of straw pricking their bare bottoms and the backs of their thighs. Obediently they sat, their knees drawn up primly together, and within two minutes they were bound hand and foot, haltered at the neck like Feely, and tied to the same post, their bare shoulders rubbing in comforting intimacy.

Their captor knelt, held the lantern so that its light fell mercilessly on their nakedness, and took a long, lingering look. They hung their heads, remained shamefully silent, then whimpered in fresh alarm as he jerked each head forcefully up in turn and peered absorbedly into their tearstained features. He nodded in slow, mumbling satisfaction, picked up the lantern, and descended, leaving them in almost total darkness.

'Should we scream for help?' Possy suggested desperately, but Feely's dark head shook.

'No, I nearly lost my voice trying. All that happened was that he came and beat me. Then... then...' the anguished sobs came welling up, and they waited until the storm of her weeping faded.

'How the hell did you come to be up here?' Possy asked, and then she was forcefully reminded that it was entirely due to Feely that all three were now in this perilous situation.

The tears came again, adding to the pathos of Feely's sad tale of betrayal. 'Guh – Gordon. He – he – I thought – we – were – he loved me—' there was a pungent interruption, until it was made clear in no uncertain terms that all three girls had been seduced by the glib-tongued and extremely accomplished lover and liar. Then Feely took up her sorry story once more.

'When the attack came, and after the engineers turned up, Gordon said it would be better if we didn't report straight back; that he'd be in deep trouble. Probably get court martialled, and that we had to think of something. We drove around, got right off the beaten track, and ended up at this farmhouse. I found out Gordon knows these people somehow. He brought me up here...' her voice faltered. They could almost feel her blushing in the gloom. 'He said things would be all right. He... started to make love. Undressed me. Then suddenly he left me here, said he'd only be a minute. I thought he'd gone, you know, to the toilet or something. Then that – that creature appeared.' She shuddered in revulsion. 'He tied me up like this – after he'd – you know – done it to me!'

'Took advantage of you, you mean?' Possy's voice shook in outrage.

'Yes.' Feely's tears came harder than ever, scourged as she was by her own private torment. That skinny, smelly body, with its totally out of proportion, monstrous rearing prick. A great, cheesy, red-domed projectile, veined and throbbing. He made her handle it, prodded her all over with it, and laid its vital heat between her breasts, squeezing them until they cradled it. He pressed it to her face, forcing her to taste its slimy emission on her lips, then to open those lips, to feel for the first time that engorged mass filling her, driving in to the very back of her throat, choking... And she was sucking, tasting that musky fluid, and then he was over her, her thighs lifting around his skinny driving frame, and its hugeness was in her, rammed in to the hilt, straining her narrow sheath while she rutted in time with his fury, and came and came...

'It was awful!' she lied, and felt her sore vagina pulse with hunger even as she spoke.

There was an interval of awed, sympathetic silence, punctuated only by Feely's weeping. Then she coughed, cleared her throat. They felt her squirming around in the straw, heard her deep groan.

'These ropes. I feel as though I've been tied up here for days. You know whose fault all this is? That bastard Gordon! I hope he rots in hell for this!' All sense of betrayal and deception forgotten, their solidarity thoroughly restored, all three were united in wishing evil on his handsome, unholy head.

Chapter Eight

Betty Squires bit hard into the corner of the blanket she had stuffed into her mouth to muffle the screams threatening to erupt as the thin cane bit agonisingly into her. Her plump behind felt like a ploughed field, the flesh furrowed into ridges by the swishing blows. Another cracked into the shivering rounds, and hot tears poured from her dark eyes. 'Oh please, ma'am,' she blubbered, spitting out the blanket. 'No more, *please*. I swear – I'll tell you anything you need to know. Yes, it's true, the lieutenant was shagging all three of those girls. After he finished with me – and half the other girls in the unit, ma'am!' Betty wept, with pain and relief that the punishment was over. She was still shaking with shock as well as the throbbing torment of her flayed bottom.

Clarry felt her own damp pulse of excitement at the sight of those splendid globes, with the neat lines of the strokes welling up a deep crimson from the paler flesh. The girl's knickers were sagging across the backs of her meaty thighs, clinging about the rolled tops of her grey stockings. Unable to prevent herself, Clarry leaned forward, let her hand stray over the silky smooth inner thigh, then to the base of that tempting divide and the spongy tissue hidden at its depths. She felt the crinkled folds of the lower labia, the wiry tendrils of hair adorning its edges, the moist cleft at its centre. She probed gently, saw the marked buttocks clench deeply. Betty stiffened, gasped, but remained stretched on her stomach across the narrow bed, while Clarry's fingertips probed further, into the yielding slipperiness of the inner surfaces, led ever inward towards the funnel of her vagina.

Betty snivelled. 'I'm not – I've never – I don't…' But, to her intense surprise, she found she could, and did. Long minutes later, her tearstained face rosy with blushes, she was lying on her back, her lower body bared, her clothing cast aside on the floor where Clarry had dropped it. Her body still tingled and thrummed with the violence of the orgasm the captain had raised.

Clarry was kneeling by the bed. Her palm rested once more on the warm thigh, but this time with the assurance of its right to be there. 'You know,' she crooned, 'if it ever did come to a court martial, and you ended up in the glasshouse at Aldershot, they'd have a whale of a time with this gorgeous fanny of yours.'

Betty shuddered. 'I swear, ma'am, that's the very first time I've ever done it like this…' she floundered, her mind spinning. The prospect of being incarcerated in the women's section of a military prison filled her with dread – and after these last hectic minutes, with a shameful thrill of delight.

'Now, fill me in on Prick Postlethwaite, my dear. Names and dates; all the dirt you can give me. It'll stand you in good stead, I promise. And he'll never know where it all came from. You have my word on that.' She chuckled. 'The word of an officer and a gentlewoman.'

Gordon Postlethwaite's tortured conscience began to ease just a little as, incredibly, it seemed that he might well stand a chance of getting away with it, after all. Old Lavalle would look after Felicity all right. Well, his mind shied away from unpleasant physical details. The old peasant might get his leg over a time or two, but then Felicity was a goer, wasn't she? He might be a bit of a rough diamond, Lavalle, but what the heck. A cock was a cock was a cock – and Felicity loved cock all right. She'd proved that in their short but passionate acquaintance.

He thought of her two companions. Equally hectic. All these upper crust girls were the same. Must be those expensive schools they corral them in. Couldn't get enough of the old one-eyed snake once they'd discovered what it was for. Main thing was, Lavalle would keep her safely out of the way until the HQ was long gone. With a bit of luck maybe back across the Channel in Blighty. And Felicity might well spend the war in some prison camp. Not that she need worry, even then. She was a scorcher, and had the means for survival handily built into that furry little spot between her sweet legs. The longer she was kept out of the way, the better his chances of pulling it off. Already he had spun the colonel some cock-and-bull tale about their getting separated that had the gullible old boy half convinced.

And now, the real cream on the cake, was this dike, Captain Clarry Young, being as nice as pie to him, when he had been scared to death of the old lesbian. He was truly dumbfounded, but could only dazedly thank the fates that seemed to be looking after him so well.

'Those girls! Little sluts! No better than they should

be, and a damned sight worse! Now the other two little slags have gone on the trot. I'll see them all in the glasshouse if I ever catch up with them again. I hear Keynes left you in the lurch. Did a runner, eh? Can't say I'm surprised. I can only apologise for one of my girls behaving so badly. Come up to my room, I've managed to grab a few bottles of really decent hooch. Let me make it up to you.'

So here he was, head still spinning with his amazing luck, sitting back in this bleak bloody schoolhouse, or whatever it was, at La Fourchette, sipping a really quite decent wine with the granite-faced old bat. They'd be safely away in the morning, and Felicity and her chums would be even further behind.

His head really *was* spinning, and no mistake. What on earth was happening to him? Before he could begin to search for an answer, his chin dropped onto his chest and his mind frittered to a deep undreaming blackness.

Smiling, her blood racing with excitement, Clarry hurried to her door, locked and bolted it. Hastily, she stripped down to her khaki vest and knickers. She had work to do. She knew she had plenty of time; what she'd slipped into his wine would put him out for a very long count. She'd probably have to wait several hours before he regained consciousness, but she would be patient. She wanted him to be fully aware of everything that was happening to him when he awoke.

Oh, monumental hangover. What a piss-up it must have been, but Gordon Postlethwaite wished he could remember something of it. The pounding at his temples made him groan aloud. He would have to move. Damn, it worse than he thought. He couldn't move. Not a muscle would respond. It was as if some force was holding him down. Pain stabbed his eyeballs as he opened them, stared stupidly out along one bare, outstretched arm to the upturned hand, curled fingers, the dark circles around his wrist. He jerked, felt the bite of bonds on his skin, swung his aching head and gawped at his other arm, similarly stretched, and tethered to the other end of the iron bed-rail. With searing effort, he lifted his leaden head, stared over the expanse of his pale body, saw his ankles, widely parted, also tightly bound to the lower corners of the bed. The dark patch of his pubic hair stood out against his pale skin. He saw the furled and hooded shape of his penis nestling shyly along the crease of thigh and belly.

'Hello, Gordon, my priapic little warrior. So glad you're with us again at last.' He blinked at the semi-clad bulk of Captain Young sitting in the armchair beside the bed. Saw her bare, solid legs, crossed, a horny bare foot swinging idly.

He blushed at his helpless nudity, and the knowledge that she had been sitting there, studying him at leisure for Christ knows how long.

'What the fuck?' He blinked again, the pain rolling around his skull, and prayed that he would wake now from this unpleasant nightmare.

'What the fuck indeed, lieutenant. Or rather, who the fuck? Who the fuck out of all my girls haven't you fucked? Apart from me.'

Full consciousness of what had happened returned, flooded him, and he struggled madly, setting the bed creaking, painfully burning his wrists and ankles and getting nowhere at all. 'Let me go, you crazy fucking dike!' His voice cracked.

'You can scream if you want to, Gordon. I'm sure someone will hear eventually. Then they'll all come running. And what a tale we'll have to tell, eh? You and me both.' She reeled off a comprehensive list of names, dates, and places. 'That's who you've fucked, Gordon, to be precise. Talk about fraternising with Other Ranks. That'll keep you in jankers till hell freezes, I should think.'

'Let me go!' He heaved and the bed shook. But his voice was quieter, more of a sob than a shout.

'I'm about the only one you haven't shagged – yet,' she added significantly. She stood, and his eyes bulged as he watched her slowly pull the vest up and off, then slide the pants down and step out of them. 'There, no need to be embarrassed any more. Now we're both as bare-arsed as nature made us.'

She moved close and he cringed, stared up at her appalled.

'Get off me,' he whispered feebly.

'Oh, come on, Gordy. No female can resist you, you know that. I'm wetting myself already with desire.' She pulled a rueful pout and directed her stare towards his wrinkled prick.

'Can't say you look too pleased to see me, though. Perhaps you need rousing a little. Some do, don't they? A little foreplay.'

She straddled his thighs, kneeling up, facing him. She bent and he felt the damp tissue of her vulva and the scratch of her pubic hair slide down his limbs as she leaned forward. Her wet, warm mouth fastened on his left nipple, sucked greedily, drawing the tiny point to rubbery erection, licked delicately at it with the tip of her tongue. Then took it daintily between her teeth, and nipped. She increased the pressure, bit down, and felt his trapped body jerk, the pain knifing through his sensitive flesh, and he yelped. She switched to his other nipple, gave it the same slow treatment.

When she straightened up again he was whimpering. 'Let me go, please.' His voice was a husky, submissive murmur, and her whole frame shivered with a deep thrill.

'Now let's have a look at this famous dick of yours,' she purred.

He gasped at her touch, though it was as gentle as if she were handling eggshells. She drew down the thick collar of foreskin, saw the head of the helm peep out, the slit glistening snail-like with fluid. A quiver like that of some terrified little creature transmitted through to her fingers. She began to work him with her fingers, up and down the soft, tiny column, until the beating intensified, it thickened, gave signs of growing a little harder, the muscle spasming. 'Why, darling,' she lisped, fisting him harder and harder. 'You do care, after all!'

The short nails of her other hand sought out the crinkled skin of his balls, grazed at them, and his prick jerked responsively, grew bigger and stiffer. The column was much longer now, the helm swollen, fully exposed. The shape of the veins began to stand out, and with a few more vigorous strokes she brought him to full erection. She bent, savoured the yeasty man smell of him, her nostrils inches from his rearing weapon, then she stretched her mouth, took in the glans, and bit down on it. The throbbing hard-on died magically, she heard his shrill yelp of horror, and the laugh vibrated deep in her throat as she held him, clamping down just slightly, instead of the flaring agony his reeling senses expected. She pulled her face away and held his lolling, elongated softness in her hand. She chuckled deeply.

'Why, Gordy, you've gone soft on me, dear boy.' But she worked on him again, with both hands, rolling him like dough between her palms until he was once more achingly erect, his column jutting up, a good six inches of rampant prick, the helm swelling mightily, purpled and dewy with his juice.

In spite of his weeping shame his body was as rigid as his penis, so near to coming now that he thought it inevitable, hovered on the brink of its fierce release, so that he gasped anew when she abruptly left him and climbed off his pinioned frame.

'Now, Gordon, darling, I know you won't knowingly shout. I know you don't want to interrupt our little rendezvous, but you might get so carried away at this next bit that you might cry out in sheer ecstasy. So we'd better take some precautions, yes? Look, you've even got me dripping me with pleasure, you sexy thing!'

He gazed in horror as she bent and retrieved her khaki knickers. Splaying her legs inelegantly, she wiped comprehensively at her sex, then held up the garment. 'Maybe not the dainty little unmentionables you're used to, but soaking with passion nonetheless.' She thrust them against his lips, which pursed shut with fastidious repugnance, until she pinched his nostrils sharply and he was forced to open his mouth to breathe. In a trice the undergarment was wadded irremovably inside, efficiently gagging him.

And he soon knew why.

She turned away again, only to pick up her swagger stick, and then seized the end of his prick with her left hand. To his growing terror his tumescence refused to die. When the first cutting blow was delivered, about halfway down the throbbing column, the effort to scream made his throat ache. His erection soon faded, his prick slimily shrivelled as though it wished to disappear entirely, but by that time it mattered not. She let it go and struck cruelly at the entire area of his genitals, the cuts falling across that pitiful little appendage and across the shrinking tight balls beneath, until his entire lower belly flamed with unimaginable pain.

He was sobbing, swooning, choked with his own dribble, soaked with saliva and sweat and tears. He was only semi-conscious when she swiftly untied his ankles, flipped him over so that his arms were crossed and he was kneeling, lost to everything except that gnawing, throbbing fire at his vitals. He whimpered behind the makeshift gag even at the soothing touch of a wet cool flannel, held in place over the tortured mess.

It took a long while for the pain to recede to a level of agony which allowed him to be aware of what was happening in his terrible little world, and when he did, he trembled in an almost fatalistic acceptance of his final pain and degradation. She seized his lank hair, jerked his head round so that he was forced to see her, to know what was about to be perpetrated on him. The dark patch of her pubis was now hidden by what looked like a shiny triangle of hardened leather. Two dark thin straps snaked round the join of hips and belly, holding this firmly in place, and from the centre of this shield projected an implement that filled his bugging eyes with new dread; a polished ebony phallus, curved slightly upward, quite sharply pointed at its nose, thickening substantially down towards the base. It was not shaped in any realistic imitation of a human prick. There was no swollen helm, no unevenness in its shining surface. It jutted like a rhino horn from below her solid belly.

He was crying weakly as she slowly and methodically laved the cleft of his backside with a cold cream, pressed insistently into the cleft, found the pulsing little mouth of his anus, forced a finger into the tight resistance to smear the entrance with the cream. His balls and penis ached abominably, the tears rolled down his cheeks. He made no effort to resist as she knelt behind him, drew him up by his slender hips, parted his feet and stationed herself between them. But when he felt the cold inhuman object nudge relentlessly at the crack of his backside, the little fissure of muscle involuntarily struggled against its conquest, in spite of his shattered will. Bit it was a struggle that could not be won. Remorselessly the tip drove on, gained a fractional entrance, then inexorably burned its way with ever increasing victory into the invaded shaft.

'Goodbye, my little virgin!' she murmured, her weight folded over him, as she felt the sudden yielding, the long slide into him, and shuddered herself with orgasmic thrill and longing at her triumph.

Chapter Nine

'Oh no, not me again!' Olly groaned, but her croaky murmur was one of apathetic resignation.

Lavalle grinned his yellow fanged, gap-toothed grin. '*Oui. Toi. La jaune, le noir, et le rouge!*' He nodded at her loins.

Even she understood that much. The yellow, black, and red. That was how he dubbed them, by the colour of their hair. And not just the tangled mess adorning their scalps! It must be her turn again; she felt him behind her, untying the end of the halter from the post.

'Leave her alone, you brute!' Feely protested vehemently. Every time the unsavoury character picked one of her companions to satisfy himself with, Feely was stricken with remorse. It was her fault that they were in this predicament.

'Save your breath, Feely,' Olly told her wearily. 'Don't get him mad. He'll only beat you – or us,' she added significantly.

Leaving her hands and feet still bound, he scooped her up from the dirty straw and staggered with her in his arms over to the far corner of the loft, where he had thrown an evil smelling mattress to add to his comfort. She sighed with relief when the rope at her ankles was untied, even though the initial flow of blood to her dirt-encrusted feet was painful. Ashamed, hoping that the other two wouldn't hear her, she parted her legs at once, as though eager to receive him, and whispered pleadingly, '*Mes mains, s'il-vous-plait?*' Her eyes were huge, begging, and with a grunt, he reached behind and released her throbbing wrists. She sighed gratefully and lay back, her knees drawn up and thighs well spread, while he fumbled out of his ragged trousers and disgusting yellowish drawers.

She smelt the stale odour of his unwashed body, stared at the long column of his prick, with that vast red dome shining with his excitement. To her chagrin, she felt her own tight fissure spasm, making its moistening preparations for the invasion. With a sense of shock she realised she was no longer even sore down there, that her sex was pulsing with its rebellious, eager anticipation. An anticipation relieved as that slimy dome nuzzled, probed, and easily sank into the gripping territory it had already claimed several hectic times.

The coarse rasp of his pubes slammed against her belly, pressed against her own small fleece, and she brought her knees up further, seized him with her accommodating thighs about his pounding hips, found herself thrusting back to meet his furious onslaught. Her hands came up automatically and cradled the rough texture of the jacket covering his shoulders, and she felt the slow sweet torment of her climax already sending its remorseless signals through her slender frame.

And both Feely and Possy were equally used to this satyr's frantic attentions. He was very fair about using them in turn. Usually at around this time, as the mild May evening settled in. Afterwards they would be fed, although for the first couple of days he had refused to untie their hands. They'd had to endure sitting there, having the watered down wine poured down their throats by his filthy hands, the soup or meat and vegetables fed to them from the spoon he held. He made a great thing of it, slobbering with delight, his evil face inches from theirs, letting the greasy mess dribble down their chins, between their breasts, just so he could wipe it off.

'We stink, you must let us wash... *laver*!' Feely had cried, and Olly blushed even now at the memory. He had brought a bowl of old water, some rags, and a bar of rough carbolic soap. And he washed them; their spluttering faces, their breasts, and then all over, making them kneel, their ankles and wrists still tethered, his hands slimy with soap, ferreting in between their thighs, his calloused fingers probing, rubbing, the cold rags sponging them down – like animals!

But worse was to come. He brought a stinking old bucket, hauled them up and sat them on it like putting a baby to the pot.

'We can't do it like this!' they squealed in tearful outrage while he knelt beside them, that leering grin stamped on his stubbled features. It was mortifying to find that they could – must – at least manage to dribble a stream of urine.

'I'll stay constipated till I explode!' Possy sobbed helplessly, but at least that particular nightmare had been alleviated. After he enjoyed their pliant bodies a few more times, he mellowed. At Feely's humble request he now actually brought them buckets of clean water, soap and towels, as well as the lavatory pail and, after untying them, left them alone to carry out their ablutions, though they knew he was stationed down below near the doorway to the barn, shotgun in hand.

He even covered them with blankets now when he bedded them down. It was still cold, despite the clement weather. And apart from that, Olly was terrified – and the others were too, she reassured herself, though they were a bit better at hiding it – at the rustlings and scamperings all around them at night. They managed to huddle together, piniored limbs drawn up, fitting spoon-like into one another. They let her be in the middle. She had always been the baby, the least robust of the trio, even though age-wise they were all within months of each other.

They talked; sleep, except in disconnected snatches, was impossible. They talked fondly of all the times they had shared. Talked too, eventually, about the most painful recent past and their shared unfaithfulness. 'I couldn't help it. I wanted to tell you, but he made me promise. He said we would, when we got back to England, get engaged. But that he'd be in terrible trouble, ruined, if anyone found out.' Their tearful accounts were identical, their mutual forgiveness unanimous. And they tried to boost their morale, keep up their flagging spirits in the surreal events that had overtaken them. 'They're bound to be looking for us. There must be an almighty stink. They can't just leave us... not here...'

And yet, Olly thought, the black cloud of despair looming like rolling fog over her thoughts, it has been so long, now. Days, and nights...

Not even the cloud of despond, or any other coherent thought, was proof against the delicious fire spreading throughout her now, centred on that mighty prick stabbing away at her vitals. His discharge gushed, flooded her, she rode desperately, battering her belly up, shattering herself against his male hardness, and screamed at the bliss of coming, her pretty feet sawing the air, her heels hammering on his lean backside.

Feely woke, blinking at the unaccustomed stab of light in her eyes, for it was not yet daybreak. For a numbed second, she had that lost sensation, then memory flooded back, along with the acknowledgement of her aching bones, the agonising stiffness of her limbs and the bite of the searing bonds, the chafing soreness of the noose round her neck, the sealing film of grit covering her entire skin. They struggled, shuffled apart, groaning with returning awareness as the blankets were dragged from them. Now two dark figures appeared, kneeling, focusing the beams of their torches on the pale figures.

The girls began to sob with relief. 'Oh, thank God. Please, we're English! Soldiers! Help us!'

'*Tait-toi*!' They gaped at the brutal command to shut up, stared at the newcomers, recognised the stale body smells, the ragged clothing. While their reeling minds were still taking in this information, Feely and Possy felt themselves being stretched out, hauled by their ankles until they were laid flat on their backs. Rough fingers scrabbled with the tight bonds, unshackling their cramped lower limbs, leaving their wrists tied behind them, their necks uncomfortably squeezed by the halters. The looming shapes hovered over them, there was a rustle of clothing, and from the depths of their unsavoury garments two enflamed and rigid male organs jutted.

The girls' feet were planted far apart and the bodies descended on them, with a force that knocked the breath from the captive figures. There was an anguished interval of furious jabbing, the wet heads of the pricks skidding off their inner thighs, poking at the scrub of pubic hair capping their mounds, then cruel fingers delved, plucking at the soft tissue of vulva, parting it, forcing a way for the rampant pricks to enter the unready sheaths. Unready, not for long – such action was all too familiar. The slippery surfaces yielded, took in the invaders with gripping welcome, in spite of the suddenness of the onslaught. Though the stabbing pain was extreme, the conquered sexes were beginning to respond with their own electric signals of co-operation when, with appalling abruptness, the congress came to almost simultaneous conclusions as each assailant spurted in fierce consummation.

All the while a newly terrified Olly had lain there, between the two coupling pairs, buffeted by their violent movements and listening to the grunting ferocity of the encounters. She gasped in shock as an arm shot out from the figure which lay on top of Feely, sought for and grabbed the top of Olly's thigh, the hand sliding up the smooth inner surface until it lay on the pout of her vulva, crowned with red curls.

'*Tu es le premier le prochain fois, ma petite*!' You are first next time, little one! her reeling brain tardily translated.

The two recipients of this unexpected dawn love-play were still recovering their wits when the men disengaged and buttoned themselves up. By the flickering light of the torches the girls discerned that they were much younger than their captor. No older than themselves – if that. There was an air of sheepishness about the way they hastily retreated, scarcely glancing at the naked figures as they retied their slim ankles, and they almost fought to be first back down the ladder, leaving the astonished girls in the grey gloom of the breaking day. But down below there was an outburst of cursing and shouting. They recognised the gruff tones of their gaoler, and the lighter voices of the two visitors. Then there were the sounds of hard blows, louder curses and imprecations, all of which receded out into the yard.

The hubbub faded, though more voices seemed to be added to the argument, and the girls lay anxiously, awaiting events. The day promised to be different, but they took no comfort from the thought.

'Did you notice?' Feely whispered presently. 'One of them…' she blushed fiercely in the dawning light, '…the one that had me, looked like our fellow. His son, I'd say.'

'Oh,' Possy moaned, striving valiantly for humour, 'now the whole sodding family's going to share us!'

Meanwhile, they realised they were going without their early morning meal, not to mention the washing and other facilities they were increasingly in need of.

The heat of a bright morning made itself felt in the dusty, dancing beams filtering through walls and roof before their long wait was ended, in dramatic style. Again there were feet on the ladder, the girls already expelling their breath in sighs of relief, when a new head appeared in the opening, even more startling than their last unexpected visitors. It was a female; shawled, aproned, clad in a black voluminous peasant's dress that hung to her stout, dusty boots. She was thin, her lined face suggested at least middle age, though at the moment it was hard to tell, for her unprepossessing features were stamped with a look of vitriolic fury and disgust at the spectacle of three naked females.

She was bearing a besom; a broom fashioned of a thick cluster of twigs fastened to the central pole. Even as the girls were sobbingly begging for help at her appearance, she began to lay into them, thwacking the broom down on any portion of their pinioned bodies she could find. Squealing in fright and pain, they squirmed and rolled in the dirty straw in an attempt to escape the vicious attack. However, the short halters denied success, and threatened them with imminent strangulation should they persist. Nor could they move their arms to shield them from the worst of the blows. All they could do was roll on their fronts, and thus offer the tempting vista of shoulders, backs, haunches and thighs, of which their aggressor took immediate advantage.

The home-made birch slammed down in a flurry of blows until their dusty pale skin was rosy, though the majority of the strikes soon centred on their clenching bottoms, which seemed delightfully sculpted to receive such attentions. Indeed, the hysterical fury of the beating soon modified as the peasant woman began to savour her task, and the blows fell with more deliberation and aim. She was rewarded by the shrill screams of the victims, whose behinds glowed, the twigs making a myriad pattern of angry scratches like the claws of a demented animal on the pale surfaces.

The uproar widened. An audience appeared, consisting of the youngsters who had so lately sported with Feely and Possy, then the wicked fellow who had been their keeper for so long. It was soon evident that this was indeed a family gathering, that the shrew belabouring their bottoms was none other than their gaoler's wife, and the younger fellows his sons. Whatever their feelings about their male assailants, the girls were deeply relieved when they finally persuaded the woman to cease her personal attack. The girls lay shivering and weeping, their bodies throbbing with the pain of the beating, while the verbal dispute went on unabated over them.

It ended with the girls being summarily untied, on the orders of the wife, whose savage tongue-lashing was almost as deadly as her physical efforts, for the menfolk hastened to do her bidding. They scuttled away when she dismissed them, and the girls gathered that she was shocked at the fact of their nudity in front of her husband and offspring. Then the wife gestured for them to wrap themselves in the smelly blankets before proceeding to climb down the ladder. Eyeing the broom, which she still clenched menacingly, the three figures obeyed as cravenly as the men had seconds before.

Their hopes that their imprisonment was over were soon dashed, however. At the back of the rambling farmhouse they stood sheepishly in the strong sunlight, blankets draped over their shoulders, while the two sons filled a tin hip bath with hot water, then were dismissed, with dire warnings about trying to peek from a distance. Somehow, the girls thought, the lads would not disobey.

One after the other the girls climbed into the narrow bath and sat, gratefully scrubbing themselves with the soap and flannels provided. The woman was able to issue her orders by means of vivid gestures, and the broom added eloquent meaning to her pantomime. They struggled to empty the heavy bath into the outside drain, then lined up and washed their hair in the bowl laid out on a wooden bench.

Dried and unbelievably sweet and clean, once more covered with the coarse blankets, they obediently filed inside the building, and sat in a row on a low wooden bench in the large stone-floored kitchen. Here the farmer stood guard over them while his wife disappeared, but now the looming priapic monster who had reigned over their bodies so fiercely was reduced to an unshaven, shifty, furtive individual, who warned them with raised finger to cavernous mouth and many nervous shakings of the head as he pointed first to them, then to his own loins, to say nothing of the nightly diversions he had practised on them.

His wife reappeared, and sent him on his way with a stream of clearly uncomplimentary verbiage, from which they guessed that she had a fair idea of what he had been up to without their corroborating evidence. She flung at them three shapeless smocks made out of a material so scratchily coarse it could only have been used originally for flour sacks. Nevertheless, they pulled them quickly over their heads, thankful for even such ugly garments to hide their nudity. There were no underclothes, nor any footwear. They dared not mention their own clothes, which had been taken from them so long ago, it seemed, though both Olly and Possy had

had a comprehensive wardrobe stowed in their kitbags in the rear of the car. Of which there was no sign, either.

They sat at the table, were given bowls of cold gruel and hunks of rough bread, and a plentiful supply of cold water to drink. After that, the woman assigned them to their tasks about the house. Cleaning first, then peeling vegetables, before being taken to the upper storey to make beds, sweep and dust, then gather up seeming mounds of clothing, take them out into the sunshine and wash and rinse them in the wooden tubs. The sun was past the zenith before the clothes were pegged on lines and draped on convenient bushes to dry. Next they were made to gather up buckets of an evil-smelling swill, and take them over to the reeking sty to pour into the troughs for the fearsomely big, grunting swine. Then the hens to feed, the large vegetable patch to dig, later to water, all carried by bucket on a long trek to and from the well in the muddy yard.

They cooked and served the evening meal, standing by while the family ate. Only after they had washed the dishes were they permitted to sit and eat their own repast, after which they had to clean the kitchen once more. It was dusk before they were at last finished, and hastily sluiced down face and hands outside the back door, in the rapidly fading light. Three prickly, straw-filled mattresses were flung on the cold kitchen floor. This time it was the wife who stood alone over them and ordered them brusquely to take off their shifts, which she gathered under her arm and put to one side. When they lay submissively down, she tied them pretty much as her husband had done, by wrists and ankles, and with halters around their necks that were bound securely to the adjacent solid table leg.

'*Bonne nuit. Dormez bien,*' she announced, before blowing out the lamp and marching up the stairs where, presently, they heard the bed creak as she clambered in beside her husband.

'Good night, sleep well?' echoed Feely passionately. 'I feel like poor Cinders.'

'I almost wish we were still out in the barn with old monsieur's randy goings-on to contend with,' Olly muttered, and the silence from her two comrades at her scandalous remark showed they were by no means as shocked as they should have been.

Chapter Ten

The May days changed to a glorious June. The war seemed to have passed them by completely. Indeed, they sometimes had the feeling that the rest of the world had somehow mysteriously disappeared, leaving only this backward, out of the way spot, surrounded by the low-lying scrub and tall, distant rows of trees. But occasionally they would catch faint rumbling noises that could not possibly be thunder, and distantly droning dots of aeroplanes became a common sight in the unfailingly blue sky.

'We ought to try to get away,' Feely muttered softly, more than once, as they performed their endless chores, and the other two would share her piercing shame at their lack of spunk, as they saw it. On the other hand, they comforted themselves, how could they? They were seldom left alone, never beyond easy reach of at least one of their captors, for their gaolers had now increased to four. And in their snatched discussions and whispered confabs during the hours of sleepless dark on their mattresses, they acknowledged the formidable difficulties they would face even if they did manage to escape from the farm. No money, no papers, not even a pair of knickers between them! And the British, they suspected, long gone. No, better for them to wait to be rescued, for the British and French forces to drive the Huns back once more, rather than risk venturing so ill-equipped into the chaos beyond their enclosed world.

At least their sexual slavery had diminished. Not dissolved entirely, as they thought it surely would be, once they came under the tartar regime of Mme Lavalle. To their chagrin, they found that the fearsome matriarch had a strange moral blind spot as far as her two teenage sons were concerned. A weird ritual was established whereby, with her full knowledge, indeed, at her consent, the girls would take it in turns to mount the creaking stairs at night and get into the wide old bed the boys shared, there to spend an hour servicing their insatiable appetite, before an imperious thudding with a stick on the floorboards of the master bedroom declared curfew time, and their chosen object of lust would have to detach herself and be led back down to her fellow prisoners, where one of the boys would tie her in place once again before scuttling back upstairs.

The girls were never allowed to operate in pairs. Only one made the journey at a time, had to face the clutching, writhing masculine bodies in the stuffy dark, make herself available to both, the senior son taking precedence over his brother, who would climb aboard immediately after his older sibling had rolled clear. The girls confided few of the details of these encounters, professed a delicate disgust at being used thus, though in truth, they were usually ready for that second assault, generally achieving the ultimate sensation of their own release only during that second coupling. At least, for the first few nights of this regime. Gradually, emboldened, the girls managed to slow the haste of the sexual manoeuvres, to teach both sets of grabbing hands, searching mouths, the joys of deliberation, the dizzying foreplay which made the whole experience so much more meaningful – a lesson for all five young people from which their education benefited greatly.

It was poor glum Lavalle senior that the girls began to feel sorry for. He grew more stooped, more woebegone, with every passing day and long night, for he was denied any opportunity to be alone with them. They began to suspect that, upstairs in the long nights, he too was haltered to the bedpost as they were. So perhaps it was his frustration that made him carry out the drastic move that led so suddenly to yet another fundamental change in the direction of their young lives.

They were awakened from uneasy slumber by an unaccustomed clatter. They heard the shrieks, then the pounding of boots on the stairs. The blankets were plucked from their naked frames and the girls yelped at the frenzied attack with the faithful broom, as madame laid into them with what seemed a nostalgic desire to recapture the excitement of that first distant assault. But it was merely to seek an outlet for her agitation. Minutes later, safely clad in their shifts, snivelling as they massaged their stinging rears, they learnt that her husband had vanished.

Somehow he had spirited himself away from her sleeping side, not, as she had fleetingly suspected, to plough one of the English harlots, but to escape the environs of the farm itself.

He was missing all morning. In an atmosphere of increasing foreboding the girls went about their chores, but everyone was waiting tensely for something to happen.

In the early afternoon of shimmering heat, the air was

disturbed by a mechanical rumble, and emerging from the screen of trees, wending their bumpy way along the track at the end of the field, came two vehicles in an unfamiliar shade of grey, but clearly military. The first was a box-like car, with canvas roof and no windows, the second a truck.

They could see helmeted figures, then with a sickening lurch of hearts, the girls saw the black crosses edged in white, the mark of the German army.

They stood rooted to the spot as the two vehicles rolled up to the grass fronting the farmhouse. Lavalle climbed out of the car, already bowing and scraping, one hand ridiculously outstretched, ushering an officer in field grey uniform towards the open-mouthed group awaiting them.

'Good afternoon, ladies,' the officer said, in accented but clear English.

The speechless girls could only assume that Lavalle had been given a substantial reward for handing them over, or that he hoped to curry favour with the invading forces, and Feely was quite sure that he had already been paid a considerable sum by the perfidious Postlethwaite to hold her prisoner.

They discovered later that the German forces had been in the area for several days before Lavalle had given them up, and that the British army had been driven swiftly to the coast of northern France.

'By now, most of them are killed or captured,' the officer told them. 'You were very wise to run away when you did.'

'We didn't run away!' they chorused indignantly.

He shrugged indifferently. 'Whatever. The problem

is that you did not surrender yourselves to our forces. That makes it difficult. You see, you have shed your uniforms and assumed the life of civilians. That makes you spies. That means, regretfully, you will be shot.'

They stared at him, aghast, the colour draining from their faces. 'P-please!' Feely stammered, clutching at his sleeve. 'We've done nothing wrong! Y-you can't...'

Beside her, Olly gave a pitiful moan and sank to the dusty ground, curling into a tight ball and sobbing piteously.

The officer stared down at her contemptuously, prodded her shaking form with the toe of his boot. 'Come, we are at war. What did you expect?' He paused, his expression of disgust at such cowardice fading as he studied their slim young beauty, evident even in the unbecoming garments they wore. 'Perhaps, on the other hand,' he said slowly, a glint in his eye, 'if you co-operate fully – tell me everything you know. But first we must search for weapons and papers.' He kicked the weeping Olly harder.

'Get up!'

Possy, who had striven not to break down though she trembled with fear, bent and roughly yanked Olly by an arm, dragged her upright. 'Come on!' she hissed. 'Get up! Don't let the side down!' Olly's frightened face, smeared with her tears, glared up at her, a spark of indignation penetrating her terror at such a stupid statement. However, she let herself be hauled upright and wiped at her streaming cheeks with the back of a hand.

The squad of half a dozen men, under the command of a corporal, had been ogling them throughout the brief exchange, but now, at the lieutenant's rapid spate of orders, they sprang to attention, surrounded the three woeful figures and marched them off to the barn where, in their first days, they had been held prisoner. They stood the girls in a line, then faced them, stepping back a few paces. The block of sunlight fell on the drooping figures from the wide open doorway. Their heads bowed, they stared at their dirty bare feet and snivelled softly.

'I regret that this is necessary,' the officer said in his clipped tones, but the accompanying smile gave the lie to his words. He approached Possy first and knelt at her feet. She saw the high-prowed peaked hat, with its grimy dust cover, and gasped as she felt his hands on her legs, at the backs of her knees.

They slid up, over her firm thighs. One passed quickly between her legs, his sleeve brushed her vulva, fingers flickered over the tuft of her pubic hair, then the hands were at her hips, moving on, upward, and her smock lifted with his progress, caught on his forearms.

'I say!' she gasped again, her face flaming as her naked body was displayed to the waist. His hands continued their exploration, the bodice of the coarse dress straining as he cupped her soft bare breasts. To her shame, she felt her nipples tingle, harden, their little points rubbing against his touch, and she shivered. The hands slid swiftly down her back, paused slightly to appreciate the curve of her bottom before, at last, they were withdrawn and the shapeless smock fell into place again.

'Fraulein?' the lieutenant said politely. Avoiding the smirks of the men in the line opposite, Feely raised her arms out to her sides, facilitating the officer's search, which was equally thorough and revealing, to the delight of his men. 'And now, the little redhead,' he grinned, and Olly managed a feeble smile. His examination of her naked charms was slightly more lingering than the rest.

'So,' he declared when he had done. 'You travel light, ladies. Now, you talk to me. I think one by one. It is more private.'

'You are entitled only to know our name, rank, and number,' Possy answered defiantly, though her voice quavered. Olly gaped at her foolhardiness, wanting to scream at her for endangering them even further, but the lieutenant seemed in good humour after his body searches. He shook his head amusedly.

'You forget, fraulein. That is for captured enemy forces. You have nothing to substantiate your claim that you are from the military. No uniforms, no documents. Your clothing – such as it is – appears to be local. As I have told you, the conventions of warfare do not apply to spies.'

In fact, as they subsequently found out, he had everything: their pay books, identity discs, their kit; for Lavalle had kept everything, and handed it over when he decided to pass them on to the Germans. But at the time of this first interrogation, they did not know this.

Wisely, he began with Olly who, wide-eyed and tearful, tumbled out as much information as she could give, in a semi-coherent, babbling stream, which he had to keep interrupting to make sense of. The senior officers, the location of the 1st Group's HQ, the numbers, as far as she could ascertain them. Anything, from the most insignificant trivia, she poured out, in an ingenuous flow designed only to save herself – and her two dearest friends, she repeatedly assured herself when she thought over what she had done.

She even told the truth when he questioned her about the circumstances which had led to their desertion from their unit.

'We came to look for Feely – Private Keynes, sir. The HQ was pulling back and she'd gone off with… with…' He saw the deep blush come sweeping up her freckled face, and patiently raised his eyebrows, like a reproachful parent. Out came the sorry tale of love and lust and deceit, while he struggled to keep the smile from breaking out on his stern features.

Minutes later, he was aware of the whole shameful episode of Gordon Postlethwaite's philandering with all three of them, and shook his head in genuine amazement. 'So, in fact, you girls are nothing more than harlots, for the amusement of your officers?'

'Oh no, sir!' Olly gasped, her eyes round with shock. 'It was all a mistake. We were all virgins when we enlisted, sir!'

'Straight from school, you said. I should hope so.' It was clear to Lt Kleber they were telling the truth. Except for the redhead's claim that her father was an English milord. She was so terrified at his threats she had probably thought that might impress him somehow. On the other hand, though, her behaviour fitted in with all he had heard about the degenerate English aristocracy. All three seemed to come from decent backgrounds, in spite of their lowly rank.

They knew how they could best serve their country,

he thought. He grinned, remembering his own not so distant exploits with the Hitler Youth, and the beautiful girls only too willing to prove their patriotism, in so many delightful ways. And he had undergone a great many experiences since then; the past weeks had been full of danger – and heady conquests. He deserved something, after what he had been through. The spoils of war. He was not going to turn down what the fates had so fortuitously cast his way.

'I don't know whether you're lying to me,' he mused slowly, and saw the fear leap again into the girl's brimming eyes. 'You know, I have the right to have you shot right now. At such times, decisions remain with the officers in the field.'

'Oh please, sir – I swear I've told you everything. Please – I'll do anything!'

She sank down, sobbing, and clung to his dusty boots, her unkempt mop of fiery chestnut hair spilling over his knees, her brow resting on them. Gently he bent and lifted her. 'If you're very, very good, fraulein,' he whispered, staring into her eyes. The blood came up under her pale freckled skin, but this time he could see she understood exactly what he had in mind.

'Anything,' she repeated in a husky whisper, and he felt his cock stiffen in his pants at her submissive tone.

'First, for your cowardice,' he said, his voice transformed, harsh, and she nodded. He pulled her roughly over his knee and tossed the hem of the dress up over her behind. He studied the tight globes, let his hand play over their smoothness, his fingers delve into the deep crack, searching out the damp, hidden crevice of her sex, feeling the springy tendrils of her pubic curls.

Slap!

He struck her with an open palm, a stinging blow, but not too hard, and was thrilled by the rosy imprint which came up on her flesh. He watched the buttocks flinch, the deep hollows as the muscles clenched, and he struck again on the other resilient cheek.

Slap!

'Oh – ow!' Her gasped cry, the flurry of her dainty feet, the pink heels see-sawing the air, her belly wriggling against his throbbing cock, thrilled him even more. She sobbed quietly, breathlessly, yelping at each fresh smack.

Slap! *Slap*!

'Oh! Ow! Please – *oh*!'

Her bottom was glowing and his aching cock was rearing up into her squirming tummy, when he stopped. He pushed her from him and she rolled onto the wooden floor, her feet still kicking, her hands rubbing at her fiery backside.

'Please me some more,' he growled, and her squirming stopped, and she stared up at him, wide-eyed once more. He sat with legs parted, and from his open fly jutted a ramrod penis of impressive proportions. 'Your own officer has run away with all his fellows. They are all dead or captured now. Soon we will be in England in their place. Now you can pay tribute to an officer of the Third Reich.'

Olly shuddered. She knew what he wanted – was ordering – her to do. She had never done it before. Not actually *kissed* one.

He reached out, wound her wild hair about his hand and dragged her mercilessly in to his gaping thighs.

She felt the engorged head drive against her face, slide over the smooth curve of her cheek, and felt the slimy trail of fluid the tiny aperture deposited on her. Then its beating wet warmth was all over her, her lips touched the throbbing length, the great dome rested on her brow, he manipulated it against her blind face. She opened her mouth fearfully, heart thudding, poked out a timid tongue, licked at its salty tang, for the first time tasted the thick honey of the male emission. Her vagina gave a great spasm and she felt her own mini-flood between her thighs as she stretched her mouth wide and took that proud, fierce, purpling dome fully into her surrendered opening.

Chapter Eleven

'Well, my dear girls, what on earth are we to do with you?' The speaker was an elderly official in civilian clothing, though he introduced himself as General Langfeldt. The girls were conscious of his gaze moving with slow appreciation over them as they stood rigidly at attention, their arms stiffly at their sides.

Although they had been permitted to wash and had been given brushes and combs to attend to their hair, they were still wearing the same ugly shifts Mme Lavalle had forced upon them. Somehow they sensed that General Langfeldt was all too aware of their nakedness beneath the coarse shifts. After all, everyone else was, including most of the inmates and guards in the gloomy old prison which was all they had seen of Paris, having been transported there in a covered truck following the lengthy interrogations conducted by Lt Kleber.

The questioning had taken almost the entire previous night. The girls had not exchanged detailed accounts but it was obvious, even from what they had said, that their experiences were very similar. Clearly, the lieutenant was a soldier of impressive physical stamina – and appetite! It was their shame at the degree of their co-operation in their examinations that had kept them silent. If they had confided in one another, they might have taken a great deal of comfort from the fact that their thoughts had run so closely parallel. All three reasoning that whatever they had to tell could be of little value to their enemy, now that the British and French appeared to have suffered such a comprehensive defeat. But in their precarious situation the girls' eagerness to comply went far beyond military tittle-tattle. Lt Kleber seemed pleased with them, anyway, and the girls were more than a little reassured that they had found a way to ensure their survival.

And the expression in the portly general's eyes told them they were not wrong. However, they were soon to learn that he was made of sterner stuff than the amorous Kleber, and his pleasures were more robust.

When they were escorted from the dark communal cell some hours later it was not by the glowering French wardresses, but by two smartly turned out German soldiers. They marched through a succession of gloomy corridors, the soldiers' boots echoing, until eventually they found themselves in a brightly-lit basement room. It was furnished simply. A desk stood against one wall and a long narrow table occupied the centre, but it was not these plain items that caught the girls' attention. From a pipe running beneath the ceiling hung lengths of chain, and at the end of each chain dangled a thick iron bracelet. There were similar sets of restraints laid out on the cold stone floor, the chains being fixed to solid bolts.

The guards pushed them over to these appurtenances and gestured for them to stand with their feet apart, ready to be shackled. They pulled off the girls' wooden clogs and cast them aside, then clamped the iron manacles around their slim ankles. The girls began to whimper. 'Oh, please what are you doing? We've told you everything...'

But the guards merely grinned. The girls' feet were now pinioned about twelve inches apart. The two men straightened, grabbed their wrists, and within a few seconds the girls' arms were at full stretch above their heads. They were keening softly when the guards, after a last brutal grin, turned and left them trussed under the bright lights.

'Oh, my God,' Olly moaned, shaking her head, 'what are they going to do with us? Why are they doing this? I've told them every thing I know, what more can they want?'

Her words shamed Possy, who shied away from the image of her own confessional with the lieutenant. 'They're just trying to scare us, Olly. Chin up.'

'Then they're bloody well succeeding!' Feely burst out, striving to check her own weeping, but with little success.

The girls suddenly shut up and stared like rabbits when the door opened, and they saw the plump figure of General Langfeldt. Behind him came two figures, one short and young looking with flaxen hair, the other tall, stooped, with small round spectacles perched on his prominent nose. He was bald except for a greying fringe of hair around his temples. He looked like an academic, and only a little younger than the general. None of them were in uniform, all were very informally dressed with braces hooked over their collarless shirts.

'Ah, there you are, my dears,' Langfeldt beamed. 'All ready for us, I see. Well, perhaps not quite.' He sniggered, shook his head and moved close to Feely.

The chains rattled softly at her involuntary movement to lower her arms, to close her legs. 'These are my colleagues,' he went on. 'They have come to assist; we know how cunning you British can be. I am sure there are some things you are keeping back, some little secrets you would like to share, yes?' His voice was deceptively pleasant, and as he spoke he bent, picked up the hem of Feely's dress, and rolled it slowly up her body, exposing her thighs, the dark triangle of her pubis, her flat stomach, and then her breasts. Finally, he slipped it up and over her head so that it hung like a tight brace at the back of her neck and shoulders. Her naked body was fully exposed, the chains chinking more loudly at her hapless attempts to cover herself.

'Gentlemen, be my guests,' the general said, without taking his beady eyes from the beauty exposed before him. In a trice the tall professorial figure reached out and did the same to Possy, while the younger man did the same to Olly.

'There, now we can see what you are made of,' the general went on. 'Have you anything to hide?' His face was so close to Feely's now that she felt his breath upon her. She defiantly tried not to flinch from him, but could not prevent a gasp at the lingering touch of his cold hands on her breasts. His fingers pinched the resilient flesh, and his palms curved to fit the contours as he explored her at leisure. He centred on her poor nipples, taking them between thumb and forefinger, tweaking pulling and rolling until they budded to their tiny hardness.

Like spiders' touches the hands left her bosom and moved slowly, the fingers walking over her flesh down

119

to her slender waist, round to her haunches, which he cupped and explored at length. Then the right hand crawled around her hip, and the fingers plucked at the dark curls of her pubis, lifting the skin beneath, roaming at will through the tight patch to the soft pout of her mound, and the moist beginnings of her sex cleft. A finger rooted at the folds at its peak and nosed an entrance to the slippery inner surface. Feely's hips jerked involuntarily, reflexively, as his wicked fingers sought for and found the throbbing little tip of her clitoris. Her mouth opened as she sagged against the chains, and her toned loins thrust forward, helpless to resist his stimulation. She began a small rotating rhythm, moving to his circling fingers, feeling her juices starting to flow, their erotic aroma rising between them as his mouth covered hers. Her lips parted, surrendering as those other lips were surrendering; moist, pulsing with hunger, her helpless need.

She was panting, her breath wheezing, her breasts heaving when he finally pulled his mouth from hers. '*Please*,' she gasped, at the mercy of that rotating finger, her senses lost to the screaming desire he had roused in her, but his snigger was deep and cruel in its denial as he brutally withdrew from her clutching sex. A convulsive sob shook her frame as she hung, swaying gently, shivering and moaning. Her head was down, her dark hair over her eyes. '*Please*,' she murmured again, mindful of the begging tone, the shame of her exposed nakedness, and her open body.

Matters had been proceeding along similar lines with her two fellow victims. 'Gentlemen,' Langfeldt's tone was one of amusement as he reached across and smote the blond officer hard on the shoulder, and with a grunt the younger man withdrew from the enveloping clinch in which he had been holding the sagging Olly. The bald one had been much more clinical in his approach to Possy and was already standing back, his eyes glinting behind the rounds of his spectacles. 'Time for a little discipline, I think. Yes?'

The three pale figures had recovered sufficiently to observe with growing trepidation the actions of their captors, each of whom was now wielding identical instruments of punishment; whips, the black leather handles plaited, and from which dangled fine leather strands. 'To work, gentlemen,' Langfeldt invited. 'And remember, we must be firm but not entirely merciless towards our conquered foe.'

Olly began to thresh against her chains, her body writhing, her mane of red hair tossing wildly. 'Oh please,' she blubbered. 'Don't hurt me, I beg you. You can do anything – I promise – anything, only please don't hurt me. I can't stand it. I've told you all I know… I'll help in any way—'

'Shut up, Olly!' Possy yelled. 'Can't you see that's just what they want? They're loving it—'

'I don't care, I don't care!' Olly sobbed, hanging helplessly, no longer struggling.

'The blonde shows spirit,' the general said. For a second he was tempted to swap with his partner, but then he nodded. 'Lay it on hard,' he urged. The pale eyes behind the thick lenses sparkled and the tall figure nodded.

Langfeldt brought his attention back to the lovely dark-haired creature staked out so appetisingly in front

121

of him.

'Come and meet your chastiser,' he crooned, and let the thin strips of leather trail gently over Feely's delicate shoulders, over her breasts, down over her taut midriff, brushing across the tuft of pubic hair, and between her tensed thighs.

He moved round behind, saw the body twist, the head and shoulders try to turn, the sobs shaking her. At the light touch of the whip her buttocks clenched, and he felt himself achingly erect. His arm drew back, not too far and with nowhere near his full strength, and then he savoured the hiss and the satisfyingly crack as the lash fell squarely across her bottom and curled in a final stinging bonus around a jerking hip to flick at that curl-capped mound. Fine lines of red came up and he waited, listening to her heaving sobs, enjoying the writhing shape before he struck again, almost exactly in the same place, and the whirling dance began again.

Her behind, the lower spine above it, and the backs of her thighs below, were covered in an angry network of thin red lines before he desisted, only to move to her front, where he tenderly brushed the disordered hair from the tragic young face, her eyes awash with tears. She became aware of him, the contradictory gentleness of his touch, and he saw the beseeching expression in her eyes.

'Please,' she whispered, so that only he could hear her, and he knew what she was begging him for and what she was offering him instead of the pain he was giving her.

'Not yet, my dear,' he muttered softly.

He stood back, concentrated on the area of the lower

belly, the dark triangle of her mound, the front of her thighs. They shivered, the narrow hips jerked and swung in vain efforts to shield this sensitive area from his strokes. He struck more quickly now, filled with a savage joy that he knew he must curtail, aware too, of his almost spilling need.

For Feely, reality had homed in to her agonised flesh, and in particular the area where the lash bit and spread its fire, which strangely became both a torment and part of that other fire deep inside of blazing sexuality. When at last he ceased beating her she blazed with an inner fire that raged, despite the torment.

When he unshackled her she sank against the comforting bulk of his body. He gathered her up, grunting with the effort, and bore her to the long table. She was wet, ready to receive the bludgeoning masculinity of him. The scorching fires of the living weals, the brutal hardness of the wooden surface beneath her, the cutting edge beneath the base of her spine, were nothing, did not exist as she lifted her legs about his portly waist, her belly driving to his prick. Her unshackled feet threshed the air as she cried out hoarsely at the surge of the consummation, which bought their bodies together in lost and ecstatic harmony.

The girls huddled in silence on the comfortless wooden shelf they shared in the bleak cell. There was nothing to say. Each knew what the other had gone through, they shared the same experience, too shaming to be talked of.

Eventually though, Possy felt compelled to break the silence on a subject where she felt she could dredge a few tattered shreds of moral ground. Even so, her husky voice was tentative as she began. 'You know, Olly, old girl, you must try to stand up to them a little more. Don't be so – so craven in front of them. They love it, to see us pleading and begging like that.' But Possy was startled at the vehemence of the redhead's reply.

Olly swung off the shelf and strode the few paces to the other bare wall, and she grimaced at the renewed pain that flared through her body at the movement. 'I'll beg and plead and bow and scrape as much as I want if it will keep me alive and,' gingerly she touched her throbbing bottom through the rough material, 'save me from beatings like that one.' Her voice quavered and the tears came again. 'And they can shag me until my teeth drop out if that's what they want. I don't care, you hear?' But despite her outburst she was too ashamed to continue.

'Come on, chaps,' Feely put in. The altercation between her two chums had shaken her. 'Above all else we have to stick together – whatever they do to us. Although I have to say I feel pretty much as Olly says; let them do what they like as long as we come through this. And we don't have much choice, do we?' She got up and put her arms around the weeping Olly, while Possy got up and joined in their huddled embrace.

'Guess you're right, Feely, as usual.' She managed a sheepish grin. 'Sorry, Olly, old pal. Forgive me?'

At once Olly's mouth sought hers, and they kissed passionately.

Afraid of being observed through the square grating in the metal door they broke apart and lay down once more, blankets over their shoulders.

'I wonder what they've got lined up for us next?' Feely mused. She glanced about her and shivered expressively. 'I hope they're not going to keep us locked up for the duration. I get the feeling the French hate us as much as the Jerries!'

'Here you are, my darlings! Your uniforms, quick put them on. I want to see how divine you look. Come!'

The girls stared in amazement at the beautiful array of silk garments with fine lace trimmings, the snaking pairs of silk stockings of many shades, which were scattered over the wide bed. The speaker was a tall woman with neatly cropped white-gold hair. Her carefully made-up face was still lovely, the subtle signs that told of her forty-odd years skilfully hidden, her plump roundness moulded by superb corsetry to maximum advantage. At Frau Stumpf's eager invitation the girls needed no second bidding, and swiftly peeled off the plain clothing issued to them in Paris.

They still felt caught in the unreality of a dream, after their harsh treatment of the past weeks. The day after the whippings they had been summoned before General Langfeldt once more, their limbs aching with the fear of more beatings. But instead he had behaved like an affable uncle.

'We have the very place for you,' he guffawed, and though he refused to enlighten them, they felt much easier.

A week later they were moved again. A series of train journeys that took several tiring days brought them at last to the German capital, and to the smart hotel in the old quarter of the city.

'You call me, madam,' Frau Stumpf told them, with her engaging smile. She was obviously a figure of authority, used to being obeyed, but her manner was friendly, almost motherly.

And the surroundings!

Luxurious rooms, clean sheets and excellent cuisine. Their minds were still numbed by the fairytale transformation of their lives. The other inhabitants had surprised them, too; a bevy of attractive girls who smiled and waved in truly friendly fashion. It was clearly a very free and easy establishment, for the girls were wandering about in all manner of undress; in frilly nightgowns or frothy slips, some displaying even briefer undies with sweeping negligees, dainty slippers and silk stockings, and not a sign of guns or uniforms anywhere.

Shyly, their arms crossed over their breasts, the three girls slipped into the sheer garments madam offered them. Feely was given a brassiere of pale blue, the cups trimmed with delicate piping of fine lace, and gossamer thin panties of a matching shade, the legs adorned with a broader band of ruffled lace. The slenderest of step-ins about her waist, the long ribbons of suspenders clipped to a pair of filmy flesh-toned stockings.

Possy was fitted with a pair of shimmering cami-knickers in deep red, the lace edgings in black, and Olly, a similar garment in the palest cream, the lace trimming a deep coffee.

Entranced, they gazed at their images in the long mirrors that covered both walls at either side of the ornate bed. They had noted with surprise, in the short time they had been there, how many of the rooms they glimpsed had a similar display of mirrors.

Standing in their pretty underwear, they stared enquiringly at the smiling Frau Stumpf. 'What about our outer clothing?' Feely asked innocently. 'You said something about our uniforms?'

Madam's laugh was deep, full of mischief. 'And this is your uniform!' she announced happily. 'Didn't you realise? Welcome to *The Candle Flame* – the most exclusive brothel in all of Berlin!'

Chapter Twelve

Feely strained to peer over her shoulder and glared up at the tall shape towering over her. Gudrun was a black silhouette against the dazzling lights overhead. The heel of her polished jackboot ground down painfully into the cleft of Feely's bottom, already throbbing from the altogether too realistic thrashing the Danish girl had delivered only minutes before, to the vociferous delight of the select audience in the overheated room. Madam insisted they made these tableaux as real as possible, but the big Dane was getting carried away. Feely lay there, face down, Gudrun's boot resting triumphantly on her stinging bottom, while the camera bulbs flashed and the customers yelled their approval.

When, thankfully, the lights went out, leaving the tiny stage in darkness, allowing the velvet curtain to swish across, Feely sprang up, gathered up the scraps of clothing which had been stripped from her, and ran offstage to the even more cramped cubby-hole that served as a dressing room. She massaged her bottom ruefully. 'You laid it on a bit thick, didn't you?'

The striking blonde, who was several inches taller than Feely and with a much fuller figure, smiled unrepentantly. 'We must make good show, yes? Madam says so.'

Feely bit back the retort that leapt readily to mind, and rubbed her bottom. She put aside the ridiculous red white and blue drawers, the chemise, and the frilled garters, also in the colours of the British flag. Bertha, the crone of a seamstress, would quickly re-sew the cleverly designed underwear, ready for it to be ripped off the make-believe victim in the next show. Except there was nothing make-believe about her reddened bum, Feely reflected bitterly.

The shows, the *tableaux vivants*, as madam liked to call them, were becoming extremely popular at *The Candle Flame* these days. In fact, the fame of the establishment was spreading far afield, as more beautiful girls were brought in to work there. Feely was hurt, not only physically, at Gudrun's apparent desire to lay on the strap with such gusto. After all, they were both prisoners, slaves of the Nazi system. So were all the girls who worked there; French, Polish, Dutch, Scandinavian – all carefully chosen for their looks, and for their willingness to submit to the sexual pleasures practised upon them by the many clients who frequented the brothel.

The three English girls had naïvely assumed that their status as captives would have united the girls, but alas, this had not proved to be the case. Or rather, the other subject nations seemed to be united only in their dislike of the British. No doubt inspired by the French girls, of whom there were more than a dozen. The French had the notion that the British had been both incompetent and cowardly, had run away, leaving France to endure the shame of occupation. While Feely and her chums had been relieved at the news that, in spite of German propaganda, a large part of the British Expeditionary Force had escaped back across the Channel, the continental countries which had been overrun appeared to look on it as some kind of betrayal.

And their unpopularity was reflected in the dramatic interludes which madam put on. Always it was the English girls who were the victims, the butts of the jokes, the recipients of the beatings. Those silly knickers; an outfit had been made to resemble some sort of vaguely Edwardian colonial dress. The gown, the feathered hat, could be swiftly torn off, and the frilled petticoat underneath, leaving the voluminous red white and blue bloomers revealed in all their idiotic splendour. The Jerry officers always went wild with joy when they came into sight.

Baggy, elasticated legs, gripping just above the black stockinged knees, they were whisked off as the penultimate insult before the unfortunate victim was spreadeagled over the small table, naked except for the stockings and the boots, her behind prominently proffered towards the cheering spectators, and the briefly clad Germanic girl warrior laid into her with a broad leather strap.

It was ironic that the Teutonic aggressor had to be played by a representative from one of the other conquered nations; blonde, of course, which meant usually, one of the Scandinavian or Dutch girls. But there were no German prostitutes working at *The Candle Flame* – only madam, Frau Stumpf, whose benevolent despotism certainly did not extend to offering her own sexual services to any of the distinguished clientele.

Feely was sitting on the one wooden chair, in the corner of the room, removing the boots and slipping off the black stockings, when madam eased her impressive bulk into the crowded space, which smelt heavily of perfume, talc, and sweat. It was always hot at night, and under the bright arc lamps of the stage, the girls ran with perspiration.

Feely jumped up and reached for the silk robe to cover her nakedness before going up the back stairs. One benefit of being part of the stage shows was the time off for a quick bath and a relaxing drink or two in the interval, before being required to report back downstairs again. But before she could wrap herself in the robe, madam slipped an arm around Feely's slim hips and fondled her bottom. Feely exaggerated her little wince but smiled bravely. 'It still stings a little,' she pouted. 'Gudrun was a bit heavy-handed tonight.'

'Never mind, *liebchen*.' She pulled Feely close and kissed her firmly on the lips, and her tongue flickered with brief excitement within Feely's open mouth. 'I'll make it up to you later,' she cooed. 'You come to my room tonight. I'll make you forget your sore bottom, I promise.'

'Yes, madam,' Feely simpered, with lowered head, blushing enchantingly. Her body reacted, and she felt the pulsing little thrill deep in her belly sparked by the pronouncement. The girls were summoned regularly to madam's boudoir. In fact, she rarely slept alone. There were petty jealousies among the girls; boasts of special favours. But madam distributed her lesbian largesse with fine impartiality. Feely, and her two compatriots, had been recipients on several occasions in the six months they had been at *The Candle Flame*, which was why Feely's body tingled with anticipation of what lay ahead.

She no longer tried not to analyse her feelings. There

was too much discomfort in doing so. No matter how many times she told herself that she was totally helpless in her situation, that she had absolutely no choice in what was done to her, there was still that secret shame at the way her young body leapt to embrace the ignominies heaped upon it. Even the degradations of the beatings – not all performed on that brightly-lit stage, but often in the privacy of the opulent bedrooms. Many of the customers needed the thrill of bestowing physical punishment on a girl, as a prelude to making love. And even the use of that phrase made her painful inner conscience sneer at her delicacy.

Fucking, is what she meant!

There was no love in what those countless streams of men did to her.

One of the others, a Dutch girl, Lizbet, an easygoing blonde with a figure verging on the plump side, had been the only one to come painfully near the truth one grey, snow-filled afternoon when they sprawled in their habitual semi-dress around the hot stove in the large kitchen. One of the most recent arrivals, a petite French girl, had been declaiming her shock and innocence when Lizbet cut across her testimony with a cynical little laugh.

'You know why you're here, my sweetheart. Just like the rest of us. Whether we like it or not, we've landed here because we all like sex. You can deny it all you want, but we're all nymphomaniacs. We all suffer from the particular form of dementia that comes from here!' Inelegantly, she parted her thighs, pale above the tan-coloured stockings. Her robe fell open and showed her displayed crotch, covered only by the silk knickers, bordered with lace, through which the shadow of her brown pubis showed mistily. Her fingers touched the narrow strip, caressed her sex, slowly, while all around her gasps and squeals of anguished protest arose.

Lizbet chuckled, once more slowly drew her fingers the length of her proffered vulva, then raised them suggestively to her nostrils. 'Very well.' She stared round at them with a heavy-lidded, lazy gaze. 'I challenge you, any one of you. Come up to bed with me right now and I'll prove my point. And I'm not in love with a single one of you pretty cows, let me add.' The protests this time were more muted. No one took up her challenge, nor could they meet the challenge of her mocking eyes.

The girls used each other constantly for sexual gratification. Intense relationships might flourish briefly, but there was a catholic interchange of pairings that madam encouraged. She wanted her girls to be happy. 'And nobody knows better than another woman how to make a woman happy,' she told Feely philosophically as they lay entwined in her wide bed one day. 'Oh, I'm not saying you don't need a good stiff prick now and then,' she conceded, 'but for real loving, give me a girl every time.' And, at the end of the heady session that followed, the confused English girl was uncertain whether she agreed or not.

But, after the relaxing bath and a couple of restorative drinks, and with the pleasures of madam's comfortable bed to look forward to, there was still the prospect of some hectic heterosexual activity awaiting her. Slipping on her black bra and cami-knickers, the plunging bosom and high cut legs edged with a thin band of white piping, she eased her feet into dainty high-heeled slippers, drew her robe around her, tying it loosely about her waist, so that when she moved it parted to show off the full splendour of her long limbs, and moved back down to the luxuriously appointed salon which was her place of work.

She crossed to the small bar where Willy, the elderly barman, passed her the sparkling liquid in the tall glass which the customers would assume was champagne. 'Ah, there you are Felicity, my sweet.' Madam took her arm, her fingers digging into Feely's flesh in what was clearly meant to be some sort of message. 'Someone here's been asking especially for you. General Langfeldt. I believe you two have met before. Make him welcome, my dear.'

Feely blinked, startled by this link with the past, as the portly figure advanced with hand formally outstretched.

'The green room's free,' madam whispered to her. Then, raising her voice, she said, 'General, perhaps you'd like to take Felicity somewhere a little more private? Drinks will be sent to you. I'm sure as old friends you have a lot to talk about.'

In the bedroom, with the champagne, real this time, on ice, and the door safely closed, Feely felt herself blushing like the schoolgirl she had been scarcely more than a year before. Why? she wondered briefly. It was not as though she had been anything like innocent when they had last met. Involuntarily, her whirling brain ran through an inventory of men who had fucked her before this overweight, middle-aged man. Sergeant Cameron first, the perfidious Gordon, old Lavalle and his two offspring – countless times – the briefly encountered Lt Kleber. Perhaps it was not the actual coupling with this man which was embarrassing her, but the exotic circumstances leading to it; the chains and shackles, her helpless suspension, that biting whip, reaching with its fiery caresses to all those secret parts of her flesh...

She felt a tremor pass through her at the memory, and plastered a smile on as she went towards the figure who was lounging back on the pillows. She held out one of the glasses, raised the other to her lips, widening her temptingly made-up eyes as she gazed at him over the rim. He patted the coverlet beside him and she moved at once, kicking off the light shoes and curling up, nestling into his side, letting the robe trail open to expose her scantily clad frame beneath. Her nipples tingled, erect, poking their outline through the black satin.

'You look wonderful, my dear. No need to ask how you're getting on.' He chuckled, and his free hand fell to her smooth thigh, slid up the cool skin until his fingers toyed with the thin piping of the material that followed the crease of her thigh and belly. There was room enough for the hand to glide under, to disappear under the satin and stroke the springy tendrils of her pubic hair, to pinch at the padding of flesh covering her mons.

She shivered again, recalling those creeping spider's touches on her helplessly trussed body. His deep laugh vibrated through her. 'I chose well for you, my little English slut, yes?'

'Yes, herr general,' she breathed. She moved, opened her legs just a fraction, to allow his probing fingers access to her moist fissure. He traced the groove of her sex, and nuzzled through the outer folds. She gasped softly at his rousing caresses.

'I was watching you in the show tonight.' His own voice grew huskier, betraying his emotion. 'Poor little Englander. Beaten everywhere, I fear. It is your role in life.'

'Yes,' she whispered again, submissively, and he purred with pleasure.

His hand pulled away from her crotch and he rolled towards her, kneeling up. 'I'm afraid I can't resist the urge either, my sweet whore.' His fingers pulled roughly at the thin straps at her shoulders, and she too knelt, facing him. Her slender shoulders squirmed, and her upper body gave a little shimmy. Her pert breasts jiggled as she eased the silk top of the garment down, and it fell, gathering in a silken roll at her flat tummy.

'I think you'll have to help me with the rest of it, general,' she sighed breathlessly, and lay back, stretching out her shapely legs. She felt his rough hands clawing at her as he fought the fragile garment down, off her hips and lifted buttocks, dragged it the length of her limbs, off her ankles and feet. He rolled her over onto her front, and stared at the still quite visible strap marks branded across her bottom.

'Please, general,' she quavered, knowing her very tone was exciting him. 'Not too hard, I beg you. That Danish girl, she really hurt me, you can see.'

'Yes, I see,' he croaked. His cupped hands were gentle at first, stroking her, following the contours of the clenching rounds, then his thumbs pressed harder, close to the central divide, parting the cheeks, exposing the darker shaded flesh of the inner fold, the tight, hidden, puckered crack itself, and she gasped with genuine fright. Then she shuddered as his greying head dipped, and his lips very softly placed kisses on her fragrant, abused skin. His feathery tongue lapped at the very centre, at the tiny lips of her anus, and on, to the moist folds of her vulva at its base.

She convulsed, moaned quietly, her face rocking from side to side on the covers. Her brain spun, her blood thundered, both with fear and a rushing excitement that was near to crisis.

The lapping tongue left her. She felt him straighten, fumble at his clothing, then lay on top of her. She felt his turgid cock smear her with its fluid. The column of gnarled flesh lay between the divide of her buttocks, then the spongy helm drove inwards, and for a crazed second she was in terror that he was trying to force an entrance into her anus itself. But then he withdrew from her once more and began to slap her, steadily, with firm strokes. First on one cheek and then the other, until they stung and she whimpered at the burning pain, the spreading glow of it, until it became one with the fire in her belly, radiating outwards from her sex.

When he finally desisted her behind was ablaze with the pain. He rolled her over onto her back, knelt between her raised and spreadeagled knees. His prick, huge, roped with veins, glistening at its tip with his secretions, jutted over her belly. Yet, when he seized her ankles and lifted them, fitting her limbs around his waist, she was wet and ready to receive him, and his length disappeared smoothly inside her narrow sheath, which spasmed in joyous welcome and sparked the soaring orgasm that left her rutting and weeping blissfully.

Chapter Thirteen

'I've asked permission to take you out tomorrow,'
General Langfeldt said. He noted Feely's expression of
astonishment, and nodded. 'Yes, it wasn't easy
persuading madam, believe me. She guards her girls
very jealously.'

Feely did not need to be reminded of that. In all their
months at *The Candle Flame*, none of them had ever
been allowed out on their own, or to go off for private
assignations elsewhere with any of the clients, no matter
how high-powered. Any infrequent trips had always
been in a group, on excursions around the city or to the
surrounding countryside, all carefully supervised by
madam herself, with the help of the few members of
her staff. Like the venerable Willy, who looked after
the bar, or Otto, the thuggish helper whose role had
never been clearly defined but whom the girls
conjectured was a dangerous character, not to be
crossed.

Feely, her robe open, and wearing only a pair of flimsy
panties beneath, moved to where he was sitting and knelt
before him, acting out the youthful coquette for all she
was worth. She knew now just how much the general
appreciated this air of adolescent innocence. She
widened her eyes and gazed up at him. 'What? Just
me? Or are Possy and Olly included too?'

She had told him her friends' nicknames. In the ten

days or so he had spent in Berlin, he had scarcely missed a night at the *Flame*, and had sampled all three British girls' talents. With fatalistic ruefulness, they had shown one another the evidence of his by-play; their bruised and reddened buttocks, the deep stains of his finger and thumb marks on their breasts and thighs, all as prelude to his boisterous coupling. But Feely suspected, and dwelt with secret pride upon the fact, that he preferred her pliant body and lively company to the others, a supposition she felt was confirmed now, in his reply.

'No, my dear. Just you. There's a colleague of mine who's very anxious to meet you.' He laughed, and tapped her nose with his forefinger at the enquiring lift of her eyebrows. 'Now just curb your curiosity, little whore, or I'll be quite jealous.

'Come, put your mouth to the work it was made for.' He opened his legs, and her nimble fingers unbuttoned his fly and took his already stirring penis from the tight constrictions of his clothing. Perhaps he was right, she thought, as she took the stiffening column in her gentle fingers, and lowered her head, her mouth opening in homage to deliver the first feather-like kisses on the swelling dome.

Certainly, she deserved the epithet he was fond of using for her, and for her two friends. Whores they were now, skilled in many ways of arousing and satisfying their clients. As she now proved, her head bobbing determinedly, her stretched jaws taking in his rigid tumescence, swallowing as much of the throbbing shaft as she could take without choking, not even pulling away when it seemed inevitable that he must shoot his semen deep into her. She did not know whether to be glad or sorry when a hand gripped her hair and brutally dragged her face away from his rearing prick. He bore her furiously over to the bed, crashed her down, battering the breath from her lungs as he flung himself on top of her. His hand clawed, tore away the panties, ripping them bodily off her thighs. She thought of madam's anger at yet another pair of expensive silk knickers ruined, then all thought disintegrated at the mighty plunge of his penis into her, and the primitive splendour of the mad rut to their mutual fulfilment.

'This is Shaun Launcey, a good friend of mine. Shaun, meet Miss Felicity Keynes. Private Keynes, late of the British army.' The general's mocking tones failed to register as she stared into the pale blue eyes in the rugged face. When Shaun Launcey smiled, his teeth sparkled white against the deep tan of his handsome features. His curly hair was short but unruly, the dark gold curls clustered about his brow, with a hint of burnished ruddiness about them. They reminded her of Possy. He was tall, six-foot or more, she guessed, and of a superbly athletic build; broad shouldered, muscular, narrow hips. It showed even in the well-cut civilian suit he wore. There was a certain magnetism, an elemental spark that passed between them, a fundamental response deep within her. She felt the sudden pouting swell of her sex, the dampness of her labia pressing against the hugging strip of silk of her panties.

'Pleased to meet you, Miss Keynes,' he said confidently. ''Tis a sight for sore eyes you are, and no mistake, after all these Jerry glamour-pusses.'

He nodded round him at the other fashionable diners,

the elegant furred women and the immaculate uniforms of their menfolk. 'All this top brass is making me nervous.' His voice was deep, carrying a lilt of laughter. His English had the easy perfection of a native speaker, though it held just a hint of a burr.

'My father's Irish,' he explained a few minutes later. 'My ma's Austrian, so I'm kind of half kraut meself. Which is why I'm here, I suppose.'

She felt a stab of fear at his free-and-easy outspokenness, but General Langfeldt laughed smoothly. The effect of the handsome stranger on her seemed to Feely at one with the general air of unreality she was feeling. To be fully dressed for one thing, in smart woollen costume and stylish overcoat. The felt hat, the soft kid gloves she had just removed. Even the simple jewellery, the tiny earrings, and slender bracelet shimmering at her wrist, added to the dreamlike sensation.

She moved her feet, felt the pull of the suspenders on her stockings beneath the heavy skirt, the soft rasp of silk on silk as she crossed her legs. Shaun Launcey reached over to light the cigarette he had offered from his silver case, and his knuckles brushed electrifyingly against hers for an instant. Their gaze locked, and the thrill quivered through her again. She lowered her gaze demurely.

'I'm afraid I have to leave you,' General Langfeldt announced, as soon as they had eaten. 'Perhaps you could show Miss Keynes some of the sights, Shaun?' he suggested. 'I'll meet you at the officers' club. Say, four o'clock?' It was obvious that all this had been carefully planned, but Felicity was too delighted to care.

Besides, she knew she was still entirely without will. They would do with her whatever they pleased, and there was nothing she could do to alter things. So she might as well enjoy herself.

She was fully prepared for the stranger to rush her upstairs to an opulent bedroom, or to some other equally well appointed hideaway where he would have her out of her smart clothes as soon as possible. So she was dumbfounded, therefore, when he did exactly as the general had suggested, and took her on a sightseeing tour of the city, in a staff car, with military driver provided. What's more, he made no untoward moves at all, though they sat hips touching in the upholstered comfort of the rear compartment. She was not only astonished, but also more than a little piqued at his propriety, and admonished herself sternly.

Although, there had to be a price to pay somewhere, she guessed.

And when she learned just what it was she was surprised – and deeply troubled.

As they made their way through the traffic towards the rendezvous with Langfeldt, Shaun said, 'The general told me all about you, Felicity. You don't mind my calling you that? And I'm Shaun, you hear?' She blushed and nodded shyly, her demureness no longer an act. She was startled at how close to the surface the ghost of the old Felicity lay. 'I'm with Special Operations,' Shaun went on. 'I'm actually a major for my sins, though you'll never see me in uniform, and I think it's a terrible sin for you to be working in that brothel, if you don't mind me saying so.' She felt the hot flood of shame rush to her face, its heat all over her body. Tears stung her eyes and she could not speak.

'I think you could do better coming to work for me. You'll need to be trained, of course. It would take time. But you deserve better than serving as a whore for these jumped up pricks with their smart uniforms. Most of them will never hear a shot fired in anger.' As if aware of the tumult of conflicting thoughts racing through her mind, he patted her arm and laughed softly. 'At least think it over, won't you? If only for my poor sake. I'd like to see a lot more of you, Miss Felicity Keynes, and that's the God's truth.'

In the car taking her back to *The Candle Flame*, the general was not so gentlemanly. 'What did you think of Shaun?' he asked.

His hands were already groping beneath her skirt, pushing up the hem, revealing her stockinged legs, the suspenders clipped to the dark tops. She was uncomfortably aware of the back of the driver's head, and worse, his flickering gaze in the rear-view mirror. The general's busy hands moved on, his fingers spread, explored the damp crotch, pushing the silk knickers hard against her soft flesh, outlining the groove of her sex. The fingers soon worked their way past the lace frilled legs of her panties, to the melting flesh itself, stirring her until her legs twisted, her hips turned, and she pressed into him, roused in spite of her embarrassment.

'Lift up, girl,' he ordered gruffly, and biting back her tears she obeyed. With clumsy haste he dragged the knickers down until they hung about her knees, then her ankles. They caught and snagged on the heeled shoes as he removed them altogether.

Minutes later, two fingers buried deep in the musky wetness of her vagina, Langfeldt pressed his searching mouth to hers, and then his ruddy face buried into the softness of her fragrant neck. He worked her, urgent and brutal in his eagerness, and she felt her treacherous young flesh responding, beating ever more imperiously as the climax signalled its remorseless approach. But when it came and she stiffened, lifting to his caress, her body locked, shuddering in its thrilling excess, it was the handsome stranger's face she visualised, his touch she fantasised stirring the flowing storm within her.

Possy and Olly were staring at Feely in astonishment. Possy recovered first. 'What do you mean, go and work for him? What sort of work?'

Feely was angry with herself at the guilty flush spreading over her face. She shrugged. 'I've no idea, really. Some sort of office work, I suppose. Checking English language documents, that kind of thing, the general reckons.'

'Special Operations? Sounds like spying,' Olly observed. 'Propaganda and so on. They say there's several English people working for them.'

'Treason, it's called!' Possy added accusingly, and Feely's face flamed.

'Would it be any worse than what we're doing here?' she countered.

'At least we're not betraying our country!' Possy fired back.

'Aren't we? I'd say we were giving succour and comfort to the enemy, wouldn't you?'

'Come on, you two,' Olly put in miserably. 'Don't

144

let's quarrel. But Feely, don't leave us, please. I couldn't bear it.' She tried a brave, unsteady little smile. 'Splitting up the ménage? It's unthinkable.'

'Maybe I could wangle jobs for you two,' Feely offered without conviction.

'No, thank you!' Possy scoffed bitterly.

However much Feely tried to push it from her mind, she could not help dwelling on the handsome Shaun Launcey, and her fascination for him. Distraction came, however, in a new diversion dreamed up for the entertainments, and it was one in which the three English girls figured prominently.

After a couple of days of rehearsal, the downstairs lounge was packed for the first night.

'Just like the theatre,' madam enthused.

The small stage had been dismantled. In its place a rectangular wooden pen had been erected with low, solid sides. In this box had been spread a good six inches of grey, viscous, dripping, artificial mud. When the three girls appeared under the spotlights, in full-length robes which they quickly discarded, a roar of anticipation erupted, for underneath they wore identical costumes; a brief brassiere and panties, in the colours of the Union Jack. But what chiefly delighted the audience was that when the girls turned in practised movement and bent from the waist, presenting their pert bottoms to the onlookers, there, clinging to the contours of their silken behinds, was a caricature of the British prime minister, his brow creased in an ugly scowl, his jowls hanging in bulldog fashion.

The girls went through a routine of exercises, skipping and shadow boxing, as though preparing for a fight, which indeed they were, for soon they were joined by their three opponents, Gudrun, Lizbet, and another flaxen-haired maiden, in abbreviated one-piece swimsuits in the German colours. The choreographed contests could have only one outcome. The three 'German' girls soon straddled their victims and dunked them in the slimy filth.

Though the victors themselves were liberally spattered with the cloying mixture, the spluttering figures kicking helplessly beneath them were virtually unrecognisable, plastered as they were from hair to toes in the filthy stuff.

Feely, her breath driven from her by the thrusting weight of the Danish girl, once more decided that Gudrun was putting far too much realism into her attack. A searching hand seized her slime-covered hair and dragged her head back painfully, while the other hand deposited yet another mass of the foul mud and smeared it over her countenance, thereby choking off her screams.

Spitting, coughing, the gleaming figures were draped over the edge of the box, which cut into their bellies. They heard the ringing shout of triumph from the girls who held them there, which was echoed appreciatively by the excited spectators.

'Down with Churchill!'

Actions followed words, and with some difficulty because of the slippery coating, cruel fingers clawed at the elastic of their knickers, the bright colours and provocative portrait of which had long since disappeared under the layers of mud, and they were dragged down the thighs of the hapless trio. Laughter erupted at the sight of the upraised bottoms, ludicrously pale where the panties had protected them, and the quivering rounds were soon smudged darkly by the fusillade of resounding slaps delivered by the three conquerors as the finale to the edifying display.

The flimsy brassieres had been plucked from them in the first hectic seconds of the mock battle, so that the three girls were completely naked as they stood facing the raucous audience. But at least they were used to appearing naked in such public circumstances, and besides, the sealing coat of mud sticking over every inch made them feel as though they were dressed.

However, as an addendum to the entertainment, the male watchers were invited to operate the hose-pipes that were provided, so that the girls could have the thickest of the mud swilled from them before they left the arena. Gradually their pale flesh began to appear, as the streams of water washed the grime from them. And, in the midst of this, as Feely stood enduring this chilling treatment, she suddenly wished that the floor would open and devour them, or that a bomb from the infrequent British raids would land directly on them. For there, near the back of the room, beside the familiar figure of General Langfeldt, stood Shaun Launcey, grinning and applauding with the rest of them.

Chapter Fourteen

Still dumb with shock and dismay, Feely added nothing to the litany of bitter complaints as the English girls jostled under the shower to remove the residue of filth from their shivering frames. She scarcely registered the taunts of the other three, who had acted the role of victors and were sharing the same tiny space.

'That mud gets everywhere,' Gudrun sniggered. 'Here, let me help you.' And Olly squealed as the tall Dane rammed the edge of a tablet of soap deep into the divide of her sore bottom.

She should have expected his visit, Feely thought despairingly, and wondered why she should be so desolate at seeing Shaun there. After all, he knew exactly what she was. No doubt General Langfeldt had described in graphic detail how excellent a whore she was. Why should the handsome half Irishman affect her so deeply? Though her body trembled with hunger to have him make love to her, she realised that she would have been just as deeply embarrassed and troubled if she had met him as her client in the privacy of one of the bedrooms. And this thought led to another, equally gloomy.

Now that he was at the *Flame*, surely the next thing would be that she would indeed receive a summons to attend him and provide her expert services? But even as the idea scourged her, part of her conflicting mind shuddered with fastidious distaste at the crudity with which it was framed. That was not what she wanted at all. What she wanted was for them to love each other, far from all the sordidness associated with the fleshpot.

But her reflections were abruptly terminated by madam's bustling entrance. The proprietress lashed about her, and the girls squealed and grabbed for their towels, hastening to dry themselves and dodge her resounding slaps. 'Come on, my fine whores, we've got a busy night ahead. You're in demand. Hurry up! Olivia, Brenda, quick! You're wanted! You too, Felicity. The general is waiting for you.'

The next hour kept Feely fully occupied. Langfeldt was in a playful mood, and soon Feely was hanging over the end of a bed, her wrists and ankles loosely tied, her buttocks turned upward and warmed by the bundled birch the general used on her until her behind was a glowing red. His prick was like an iron rod and he was blowing heavily, his overweight body glistening with sweat when he had finished beating her. He untied her, and allowed her to crouch between his slack knees and use her mouth on him. But after barely more than a minute he dragged her roughly away from his loins, thrust her on her back, her feet waving inelegantly in the air, and skewered her with his penis, which exploded with gushing release as soon as he was in her.

She was quite surprised when he dismissed her a short time afterwards. Very often he kept her with him all night, but he sent her on her way with a mysterious smile and a finger laid against the side of his nose. 'I'm sure there are other pleasures awaiting you,' he chuckled.

Downstairs, she was even more baffled when madam waited while she sluiced herself down, then dragged her off to the tiny, reeking dressing room. 'Here, put this on,' the woman ordered. 'Special client wants you.'

There was a black suspender belt, no more than a thin strap clipped round her waist, and the long lacy ribbons dangling down. She rolled on a pair of sheer black silk stockings, so fine she could see her hand through the material as she eased them up her legs.

'No, no knickers,' madam smiled. 'Just these.'

To Feely's astonishment, there was a tiny frilly white apron, tied in a saucy bow above her reddened buttocks, the flap at the front just covering her pubic mound. There was a tiny maid's cap, also of lace, and a pair of elegant high heels completed the outfit. A tray with a bottle of champagne and several tall glasses stood to one side.

'Take it up to room three,' madam instructed. 'You're to play the maid. Be good!'

Feely glanced quickly round the crowded lounge as she headed for the stairs. There was no sign of Shaun Launcey. Probably, after seeing her literally dragged down into the mud, he had left the place in disgust. In any case, he had probably been taken there without realising what it was like, by his senior officer, which is what the general was.

Struggling against the prick of tears that accompanied a leaden feeling of despair, she climbed the stairs and walked dejectedly along the corridor to room three. She knocked, heard the call to enter, and did so.

'Ah-ha, room service at last, and every bit as charming as I had hoped!' Shaun was sitting up in the wide bed, his torso bared above the white sheets. On his right sat Olly, with Possy to his left, both girls' pert breasts exposed, making it clear that they were as naked as Shaun was beneath the sheets. Feely stood there, jaw hanging, as though paralysed. 'Come on then, let's be having those drinks, eh? We're all dying of thirst here, aren't we, girls?' He flung his arms around the creamy shoulders and pulled them to him. Under the covers, the three sets of lower limbs were in contours of entwined intimacy.

To give the lie to his words, there were at least two empty wine bottles beside the bed. Feely could tell from the ruddy features of her friends that they had partaken liberally of the contents, and were more than a little squiffy. She could also tell, and this hurt her far more than any thoughts of drunken excess, from their flushed and sated expressions that both of them had been more than amply satisfied in other ways. They smiled in that special, unfocused, post-orgasmic way which stabbed like icy darts of betrayal into Feely's susceptible heart.

Her throat closed, her eyes stung with unshed tears, and she seemed unable to draw breath. Somehow, she managed to set down the tray and pour three glasses of wine without spilling any. She even managed a brightly false smile. 'There we are, sir, I hope everything is to your satisfaction?'

'Indeed it is.' His left hand shot out, and she jerked and gasped as he gripped her squarely between the thighs. His upturned palm cupped her damp vulva and her thighs locked, clamped about the intruder as she felt his rude fingers exploring her sex lips.

'Please, sir!' she gasped, the rictus smile still pasted

to her lips. 'I'm only the maid. I'm sure you've got your hands more than full as it is. You'll find my chums here are enough for you to handle.' She slipped away, breaking free of his grasp.

'Shall I leave the bottle here?' she asked, her eyes locked with Possy, who was staring at her with curious intensity. A silent intuitive knowledge passed from one to the other. Feely crimsoned, uncomfortably aware that Possy had somehow read her disturbed mind. At the same time, the consciousness of the anguish she felt at the thought that both her friends had known the bliss of coupling with Shaun struck her, and she felt a fierce rage against them.

Shaun's twinkling blue eyes were steadily upon her, and she had the hideous sensation that he, too, could interpret her vivid emotions. Not really knowing what to do, she spun on her high heels and headed for the door, but at the last second, she turned. 'Oh, by the way,' she announced in a clear voice, 'if you still want me, I'm definitely up for that job you offered. You know where to find me.'

Feely stared down between her feet, terror-stricken, at the ground rushing up to meet her. She screamed at the top of her straining lungs, the horror of being literally booted out of the aircraft into the whirling maelstrom of darkness replaced by a new one; that she was about to be splattered on the earth she had longed to be in contact with again. The whole crazy tumble of the last few seconds stood as the perfect metaphor of her life over the past three months and more.

Plucked from the pampered security of *The Candle*

Flame, through her fascination with Shaun Launcey, and her fit of petulant pique at his choosing to bed both Olly and Possy whilst denying her, she had spent the proceeding months on a rigorous training course which made demands both mental and physical she often felt were totally beyond her. The secret location in the Black Forest was a school for secret agents – spies, as Possy had so rightly dubbed them.

Her chums had been stunned at her decision to leave, as she had herself. She had come within an ace of calling it off, but then several meetings with Shaun – intimate chats that held promise of so many more romantic intimacies to come – had beguiled her into making the break.

It was as if her life as a whore had not taken place. He treated her with a courteous affection, and without the slightest hint of impropriety. The first time he kissed her it was a gentle, almost tentative embrace, and her heart sang. He was fond of her, attracted to her, she knew. She saw the signs, felt his response to her beauty as he held her. Their kisses became more passionate, but their relationship never progressed beyond these amorous clinches. Once, he had put his hand on her silken knee, slid it up towards her thigh, then snatched it away as though the tardy voice of conscience had smitten him, while she felt her knickers moisten and her mind screamed helpless obscenities at his unexpected and disastrous decency.

Night after night she lay alone, unable to sleep, and teased her wayward flesh, fantasising about his loving, delaying with fine agony the sweet moment of release as long as she could. Afterwards, calmer, sated for the moment, she would tell herself that his forbearance was the greatest compliment he could pay her. Sometimes it worked for a while, but most of the time she went around in an erotic daze, lost in her constant need for him to take her.

She was almost glad when the initial office work came to an end, and the arduous training to be an agent took her away from his daily presence. The physical routine, punishing as it was, was a welcome distraction, as well as a formidable challenge she was determined to overcome. Somehow, success in this gruelling venture became synonymous with success in her personal relationship with Shaun. She felt that if she came through such a test of her character, she would win the ultimate reward of his love.

It had not been easy. Many times she was sure she would not make it, yet somehow she had survived, right up to the final tests. But in the freezing uproar of the aircraft, the last to jump, her nerve had failed. She shrank back from the gaping hole of the hatch, sobbing, cowering down and shaking her head. Sergeant Bruckner, who had wet-nursed them through the rigours of the last weeks, hauled her upright, clipped her harness to the line, brutally dragged her towards that black hole, her shrieks of terror whipped away on the chaotic wind outside. She felt her harness cutting into her crotch as he lifted her by the belt and spun her round. His broad boot placed firmly in her backside, he thrust her out into the night.

After all that, through her tumbling panic, she had left everything too late. The billowing crack of the opening chute, the agonising jerk as her plummeting fall was checked by her tug on the rip cord, had come too late, and the inky ground, the unfamiliar silhouette of trees, the canopy of country fields, swept up to crush her. She jerked her feet out reflexively, there was a fearful crackling and a hundred stinging stabs as snapping branches lashed her about the body and she turned her head away, crashing through the foliage of a tree. Her feet encountered something solid and an agonising pain jarred through her entire body. It was a solid resistance, which suddenly yielded and she plunged further – and then stopped abruptly.

Her head singing, she gradually became aware that the rushing sensation had stopped. The pulsing roar in her head was her own blood, the sound she could hear her terrified sobbing. She was perfectly still. Above her the ghostly tatters of her parachute fluttered in the tree in which it remained snared.

There was a squeezing pressure at her waist, oddly comforting in that it held her so firmly. Still unable to believe in the miracle of being alive, she stared about her, and saw she was immersed almost to her armpits in what appeared to be a sea of long grass. But it was curiously flattened, and belatedly she came to realise that she was firmly embedded in thatch.

She was well and truly stuck in the roof of some dilapidated farm outbuilding! And about her, the softly stirring countryside slept on regardless.

She made a half-hearted effort to extricate herself, but sank back in weak failure, the tears of relief still streaming down her grimy face. She was supposed to dispose of her chute immediately, she knew, and take cover before any observant enemy might come to find her. Perhaps they would fail her even now for that. But she no longer cared. She continued to shake and to weep, grateful only that she was still alive.

Sergeant Bruckner was the last to jump. She was probably well past the dropping zone, but he had no doubt followed her out of the plane, would have observed her landing. He would be along sooner or later to rescue her. If not he, then somebody else. She hung there, arms outstretched, oddly relaxed and passive, content to do nothing. She thought with a pang of Shaun, whom she had not seen for weeks. Did he really think anything of her? Was it really respect that had kept him from having sex with her, when he surely knew how fierce was her own need for him? She felt a sudden nostalgic longing to be back in the insulated safety of *The Candle Flame*, with Olly and Possy. At least there her bodily needs were well taken care of. And those needs, she had come to realise, were strong and constant. Why pretend otherwise?

Feely had no idea how long she hung there, lost in her musings, when she heard a noise below. It was coming from inside the barn, or whatever the building was. 'Hello,' she called cautiously. 'Who's there? Can you help me, please? I'm stuck in the roof.' The German tongue came almost as naturally to her as her own, after over a year of captivity, and then she started as she felt something tug at her dangling boot. Someone was carefully untying the intricate web of the laces, undoing her footwear. They must be trying to get her free. Of course, the heavy combat boots would have to come off. She felt the pressure at her waist as whoever was rescuing her eased them off her feet.

156

'Thank you,' she called, louder now. 'I'll try to wriggle free, draw my legs up. If you could just… what…?'

Hands were fumbling at her army gaiters, removing them, too. Now they were groping up her calves, under her trouser cuffs, seizing hold of her thick woollen socks and pulling them off.

'W-what are you doing?' she gasped, in sudden alarm at the feel of the cool night air on her bare feet. The hands moved on, up her legs to the buckle of her belt, which was unclipped. The zip fastener at the side of her trousers was pulled down, she felt the grip of the uniform trousers slacken, then the garment slid down over her hips and her waving legs.

'Stop it!' she squealed, feeling both ridiculous and frightened. With the trousers gone she kicked out, but strong arms captured her legs, pinning them together. A hand moved under her flapping shirttails, sought out the elastic of her woollen knickers and drew them down, too. 'Don't! Please!' She was crying softly, all too aware that she was now naked from the waist down, that her lower half was hanging down through the hole for her unknown aggressor to feast his eyes and hands on, which now roamed over her young flesh to the dewy cleft, then the twin curves of her buttocks, which they explored with leisurely appreciation.

The fingers delved, lightly traced the contours of her labia, parted the soft tissue, opening her slippery inner surfaces, taking possession of her, and her struggles weakened, her feet moved more rhythmically as her traitorous body took over at these unknown caresses. A fingertip slid into her vulva, found the hidden bud of her clitoris and stroked with wicked knowledge until she could feel her juices running down the offending digit, larding it with her excitement. She was close to a crisis when the finger was withdrawn, and she shuddered as it and a companion were inserted deep into the tight but welcoming sheath of her vagina. At the same time she felt the warmth of heavy breath on her thighs, then the feathery lapping of a tongue on the silk smooth inner skin, before the alien mouth smothered fully her melting sex, the tongue driving in to accompany the working fingers.

The long slow lapping strokes followed the line of her vulva, and she felt her assailant's nose driven rapturously deep into the softness of her mound. Her hips jerked, she flung her belly to meet the assault, and she screamed at the force of her coming, which had her threshing with savage joy.

And the movement dislodged her. Through a hazy bliss she felt the straw and wood scratching her ribs, her midriff, felt the mouth still clamped to her loins, felt the strong hands seize her parted thighs. Then, with a tumbling rush of debris and dust, she clattered down into the muddy shed beneath, her fall cushioned by the body wrapped protectively around her. The breath dashed from her by the fall, she lay on her side and stared in amazement at the beaming face of Sergeant Bruckner cradled between her thighs, his chin clamped firmly to the dark fleecy triangle of her pubis.

'Well done, Keynes,' he gasped, his grin wider than ever. 'You've passed your jumps with flying colours!'

Chapter Fifteen

Feely was taken completely by surprise when her companions turned on her. The four girls had just forced a silent entrance into the darkened cottage, on this, the very last of their practical tests before their passing out the following day. Their object was to subdue and kidnap the officer who was resting unsuspectingly in the blacked-out bedroom.

The intruders, dressed in identical dark overalls and black balaclavas, their faces smeared with dark paste, had successfully negotiated all obstacles, including the sentries posted below in the garden. Even the creaking stairs had not roused their quarry as they inched upward in their rubber-soled boots, so that when they suddenly sprung on her, Feely had no time to utter more than a gasp of astonishment before being pinned on the narrow bed, near suffocated by the woollen garment muffling her cries.

Before she was able to struggle she was spread-eagled, pinioned by wrists and ankles to the corners of the bed frame, completely helpless. She was at a loss to understand the totally unexpected assault. She had never been popular on the course – that had been evident from the start. The others, mostly Germans, though there were one or two Poles and Slavs among their small number, had regarded the renegade English girl with suspicion and hostility. But the senior officers, including General

Langfeldt and Major Launcey, seemed to look on her with special favour, and that had made her fellow students wary of treating her with too much open dislike.

Apple pie beds and buckets of icy water above doorways – on one horrendous occasion a well-used chamber pot – and other such childish pranks, had been more the order of the day.

But an attack like this, during their last mission, was inexplicable. The black cloth they had tied over her eyes sealed off her sight altogether, and she guessed they had no more need of darkness themselves. She could hear them moving around, and their giggling whispers. What on earth were they going to do with her? She guessed it was some sort of end-of-term horseplay, and her body tensed against the outrages she feared were about to descend upon her.

But again, to her surprise, she heard only more giggles, and a final whispered, 'Have fun!' then the sound of them retreating down the stairs. A door closed softly, then absolute silence.

She waited, still tensed, listening hard. Nothing. The long minutes passed, and she relaxed a little. Self-pity welled up.

She felt the clinging cloth wet at her eyelids, and failed to suppress the sniffling tears that flowed. Absorbed in the intensity of their final tasks, working in groups which had necessitated a great deal of co-operation, she had thought that, at last, her fellow students had begun to accept her as one of them. Her determination to do well, or at least to prevent failure, had been entirely for Shaun's benefit. She had secretly cherished the thought of his approval, and she dreamed, his love, as a reward for all the hardship.

And not only the exigencies of training; she battled mightily with her conscience, her deep sense of betrayal and treachery. And that in spite of Shaun's frequent, eloquently impassioned diatribes against the corrupt British system, its bloated capitalists, its dictatorial imperialist policies.

'Why should Britannia rule roughshod over more than half the world's population, while her own workers are forced to march on Parliament to beg for their daily bread?' the man she was besotted with challenged, and she hadn't the confidence or knowledge to argue. But she was not – could never be – comfortable with the role of traitor he seemed to think she would assume so readily. As did Langfeldt, and seemingly, everyone else.

Did they really think so little of her, that she could be so easily swayed to turn against everything she had been brought up to believe in? Evidently so. For that was why she was undergoing the nightmares of the training. To be set loose against her own country, maybe even to return and work secretly for its downfall, as Shaun's devoted helpmeet. That was the final carrot, or pot of gold, they dangled before her. That was what had kept her facing the rigours of the course, up to this dramatic conclusion.

All at once she stiffened, heart thudding, muscles locked, as she sensed rather than heard movement close by. 'Who's there?' she called, her unsteady voice declaring her nervous tension. She began to struggle, felt the bite of the ropes at her wrists and ankles, and sank back, her body shaken by a huge sob of defeat. There was another hint of a soft footfall and she had an overwhelming feeling that someone was there, standing over her. She fancied she could detect his body heat – smell him. Him? What made her assume it was a man? '*Please...*' she wept, hating the craven quality of her plea, 'untie me.'

The tears came welling up, and she could feel her breasts straining against her clothing with the force of her weeping. She stared up blindly, the soaking rag pressing against her eyelids, and whimpered at the touch of a hand on her leg, just below the knee.

The hand moved with calm possessiveness, up to a parted thigh, and on to the V of her crotch. She felt it cup her contours, press her flesh under the loose clothing which hid it. On, over her trembling belly, up to the swell of her breasts, almost disguised under the unflattering garments covering her. Almost, but not quite, as the hand pressed insistently, seeking out the fleshy rounds under their concealment. 'Don't,' she begged.

Relentlessly, with cruel deliberation, the fingers plucked at her, unbuttoning the front of the overalls, while she lay there spreadeagled, awaiting whatever indignities he chose to heap on her helpless body.

Then a thought struck her and shamefully, despite her alarm, a quiver of arousal spread throughout her frame with an embarrassingly strong memory of Sergeant Bruckner's cock sliding inexorably into her receptive vagina, that night of the fiasco of the parachute jump.

'You owe me one, Keynes,' the sergeant had whispered, already fumbling at his flies, pulling out his erect penis.

She was still wet, tingling in the aftershock of her

own orgasm, and took him in easily, opening her thighs, gripping his thrusting bulk, rutting with him, shuddering at his sexual violence, shocked at the echoes of excitement once more, despite her recent climax, when he pumped his semen vigorously into her. She felt tainted at her complicity, the readiness with which she had given herself, with no meaningless mumbles of protest, only an animal grunting of acquiescence in his fucking of her. Later, she rationalised that he was right.

She did indeed 'owe him one', for she passed her para training as he promised. After all, it was no more than she had done scores of times at the brothel, only now it was for a tangible reward, an insurance of success.

'Sergeant Bruckner?' she whispered hoarsely into the sealing blackness. 'Is that you?' She was convinced she was right, that he had arranged this last mischievous prank with the other girls. 'You can untie me. I won't fight – I don't mind you, you know… honest.'

The hands were unbuttoning her shirt, opening it to its fullest extent, revealing the lovely bosom, still hidden under the olive-coloured vest, and cotton bra. They tugged the shirttails out from the waistband of the trousers, then nimbly unclipped the belt, and drew down the zipper. The uncomplimentary matching panties showed in the gap, and fingers ran teasingly over the swell of her mons, felt the springy curls under the thickness of the cloth, felt her instinctive lifting of her loins in response to the strokes. Her writhing hip movements had opened the trousers further, exposing more of her delicious body in the drab underclothing, and the fingers worked assiduously, tracing the length of her vulva. They felt the increasing dampness, brought up the shape of her labial divide, which darkened, a token of her rapidly increasing arousal. The wet patch grew wider and she wept piteously, her body undulating in its own rhythm.

Her lips parted, shone wetly with promise as she breathed raggedly. 'Please let me loose,' she pleaded. 'I want to enjoy it, too.' Then she gasped in renewed fright at the feel of the wickedly sharp point of a knife placed exactly between her heaving breasts, just above the V of her vest. The fingers held the material fractionally away from her skin, and the knife began to saw deliberately through it, slicing easily, cutting through the stitched cups of the brassiere and on, until it and the vest lay in neatly dissected segments that were peeled aside, exposing her pale flesh and the pink buds of her nipples, erect at such novel treatment.

She felt him pulling down her trousers, until they lay in a tangled wraith around her knees. The knife got to work again, cut through them, and he dragged the shreds of cloth clear of her altogether. Now, apart from the ruined rags he'd pushed back so that they lay about her upper arms and shoulders, only the service knickers hid her nakedness. A finger hooked in the elastic, pulled it clear of her stomach as the knife did its efficient work, and the panties were gone.

The tears gushed forth now, for all at once she was cruelly aware of how ridiculous she must look, naked except for the ugly grey socks.

'Don't leave me like this,' she wept, her breasts trembling delightfully. 'Please, sergeant, undress me properly. You know what I need…'

For answer, she felt the gentlest of kisses delivered on her leg, on the soft flesh just above her right knee, and she gasped. A shudder passed through her, and she strained against the bonds to draw her limbs in, to move. The tide of her passion flowed powerfully, and she wanted to fling herself into his arms. But she remained spread out, pinned down, while that consuming mouth explored, devoured her captive body and she shook with frenzied hunger for him. The kisses blazed a feathery trail of need up the inside of her thigh, then down the silky smoothness of its twin.

The mouth withdrew, only for its magical lips to settle electrifyingly at her right breast, to take the hard little teat inside and suckle lovingly, until she was forced to scream out, to thrust the soft flesh up against the face devouring it.

But the sweet agony was unending, until she felt she must surely swoon or die from its torturous pleasure. Her other breast received similar treatment, then the licking tongue laid a trail down over her hollowed stomach, lapped at the shallow little recess of her navel, before tracing its course over the slight curve to the pouting mound, and the dark curls adorning it, where lay the melting divide at the centre of her hunger. When the lips kissed her streaming labia and the fingers delicately parted the glistening folds, she could no longer contain herself. Her belly lifting, she shook the bed, grinding her loins upward, imploring him to bring the release she was now ready to die for. 'Fuck me… Oh, please fuck me…' she babbled, her wet face threshing from side to side in her helpless frenzy.

The fingers slid into her glistening folds, sought out

the hidden little trigger of her desire, and she whimpered as the thumb flicked over the tiny protuberance, then pressed it.

There was a flowing, a release of her fluid, more powerful than anything she had ever known. She came, on and on, torn asunder by its violence, rocking, lifting, at the mercy of that finger, drawing every ounce of sensation from her as it drew the juices of her love.

At last – she had no idea how long the exquisite torture had lasted – she collapsed in limp exhaustion, yielded herself entirely to the feel of the bonds pinning her, the mattress supporting her drained body, her muscles turned to limpid water.

Now he must enter her – conquer her. All her urgent harshness gone, she whispered the words humbly, softly, in a final submission. 'Fuck me… please.'

She gasped and then held her breath as the column of rampant flesh sank into her, spearing her without mercy. It burned through her, like a stake through her vitals. Instinctively, she fought against the bonds at her ankles until her thigh muscles stood out as toned ridges. Desperately, she needed to draw her legs up, to ease that stabbing fire in her belly, that pounding crush of his pelvis battering onto her. But she couldn't, and she lay there, feeling her softest secret tissues being invaded by the rugged impalement. She lost all sense of identity – both hers and the man who was savaging her. But this was no man; this was the very spirit of masculine sexuality, as hers was the surrendered female, her body taken, a trophy to the priapism consuming it.

Feely lay there, shivering, keening softly, locked in her blindfold darkness, while outside the grey dawn came up, and the first trilling runs of birdsong started. Her body was an undefined mass of aches, the myriad torments of lying trapped and unable to move. She could feel encrusted semen in her pubic hair and on her upper thighs.

Dazedly, she reviewed her anonymous assailant, her unknown lover. Was it Sergeant Bruckner? Was he capable of such refined torture, of such artful loving, carrying her soaring to the very limits of physical satisfaction? Yet, in the cataclysmic violence of that last act had been the shameful thrill of her submission, even her inherent acceptance of his taking of her which welcomed the ropes that bound her, her blind and trussed passivity. This glimpse of the depths of her convoluted psyche was too painful to contemplate, and she tried to banish it.

A little later, she awoke from a half doze to the thumps of heavy feet up the stairs, the calling out of her name, in that beloved, dreaded tone. She wanted to scream out at him not to enter, to leave her to her violated shame, but he was in the room, she heard his vehement cursing, then the bonds being slashed from her hands and feet. With a groan and a convulsive sob, she at last was able to double up, draw up her knees, close her thighs, and huddle onto her side, to hide her nakedness from his shocked gaze, her arms folded over her chest.

'What the hell's been going on?' Shaun demanded. The taut curves of her rump faced him. 'Who did this to you?'

She turned then and flung herself, sobbing wearily,

into his arms, to cling tightly to him, her head buried against his chest.

'I duh – don't knuh – know,' she blubbered, clutching at him, savouring the feel of his arms about her. He cradled her on his knee, gently rocking her back and forth. 'I've nuh – no iduh – idea. Just hold me, p-please.'

He put her gently aside while he tugged a blanket free of the bed, then wrapped its coarse warmth around her securely, hiding her nakedness, which the tattered remnants of clothing merely served to emphasise. She was deeply touched by his apparent concern, yet at the same moment she blushed at her secret disappointment that he should have covered up her nudity so quickly and so decently.

His warm hand at the back of her head held her to his chest while her delicate shoulders shook as she sobbed, and unseen by her, he smiled to himself in the light of the dawning day, the taste of her sex still on his lips.

Chapter Sixteen

Gudrun lay back on the chaise longue and raised her long legs. She waggled her painted toenails, then parted her limbs in a wide, straight V. The blue folds of her silk robe fell away, revealing the narrow strip of lace-fringed silk covering her crotch. Through the gap in the leg of the panties, Possy could see the darker, coral shading of her vulva, with a few stray, gossamer fine, light brown curls poking through. She felt her cheeks warming and glanced away, still ashamed, even after all this time, of her own body's reaction to such a spectacle. 'For goodness sake put it away, Gudrun,' she scolded prissily. 'We're not at work now.'

This was a lazy time, which all the girls appreciated. The late morning, when they slowly assembled in the big kitchen, after their late rise and leisurely baths or showers, for the snack meal which was a combination of breakfast and lunch.

The tall Dane gave a gurgling laugh, and folded her bare legs under her once more. 'That isn't what you said the other night,' she teased, and Possy felt her blush deepen at this reference to the passions they had shared, and slaked, with each other in the small hours. It was true that she was finding her tastes turning more and more to members of her own sex.

It wasn't really surprising, though. All the girls at *The Candle Flame* used one another in such a way, their heroic efforts with their clients becoming more and more compartmentalised as the 'work' they jokingly referred to. With the customers, the girls' own satisfaction was the least important part of the proceedings – with most of the men, anyway. And with the girls, too.

Madam had drilled them well. They were purely objects of sexual pleasure for the men who, in an endless stream, possessed them.

That was how it was, how it had to be. Shocking though it was, Possy had discovered she preferred it like that. She could lose herself, lose all sense of shame or repugnance, even identity, when she was with the men who laid claim to her.

There were things she had learned about herself, her physical make-up, that she would rather not face. As a sharp reminder, she flinched at the residual stinging of her bottom on the upholstery of the chair she sat in. Shifting slightly, she let her fingertips play gingerly over the raised weals she could feel on her tender flesh. They were turning purple now. She would probably have to slather on loads of the tan make-up they were sometimes forced to use to hide the excesses many of their distinguished clientele liked to indulge in.

The redoubtable General Langfeldt had inflicted these latest scars, with the thin bamboo cane, which whistled so terrifyingly as it descended to deliver the bite of rippling fire. He liked to have both the English girls together for punishment. The previous night the naked Olly had bent at her side, their hips rubbing, heads touching on the counterpane as they lay face down across the bed and waited, bottoms clenched, for the caning. They tried to keep as still and as quiet as they could. They pretended that it was a kind of dumb defiance, their own little resistance to the subservience of their lives. But in fact, the general enjoyed their efforts more than they did, especially their inevitable failure, when the throbbing pain became so intense they could endure it no longer without squirming and threshing, and sobbing for mercy between the shrill yelps at each cracking blow.

The effect of such diversions on the general was immediately apparent. His penis stood out from his drawers like a pole, and he would fall on the nearest victim – in this case, Olly – and ram his weapon deep inside her for the brief fury of coitus. It never lasted more than a minute before he came. Olly had learned, just as all her sisters had done, and so her feet waved and her rising cries matched the bull-like roar of the general at the climax.

Meanwhile Possy lay, buffeted by their exertions, still on her stomach, squeezing her thighs tightly together to fan the throbbing urgency of her excitement, which complemented the throbbing blaze of her glowing backside, allowing a hand to wriggle surreptitiously into the hidden tightness under her belly, to pinch and stroke at her labia until she teased herself over the brink to the finality of shuddering orgasm.

There was an extra degree of closeness Possy felt both she and Olly shared with General Langfeldt. He was the one who had broken up the trio, who had been responsible for taking away their Feely. Possy's heart ached each time she thought of the angry way the girls had parted. She longed to see her chum once more; part of her longing to beg for forgiveness, part of her still sick with disgust for the way Feely had so readily accepted the calumny of becoming a traitor. And for what? Her obsession with that handsome Irish prick. That was all he was, one of an endless line, many just as virile as he was, that passed between their legs and through their lives.

As though in tune with her thoughts, Gudrun's husky voice startled her. 'I wonder how your English chum's getting on. It's ages since she left. Do you think she'll be shacking up with that Irishman? You must be jealous as hell, I bet. Of both of them!'

Possy shook her head, but the colour flooding her face told its own tale. Gudrun laughed again and gazed at her mockingly.

'Never mind, I bet she's missing the *Flame*,' Gudrun went on. 'One thing for sure, she won't be getting as much as we are. I've been doing a little research, working out some statistics. Just listen.' She caught the attention of the others, and sat up with a wicked grin. 'How many are we now? Eighteen, isn't it? And we average at least three shags a night, wouldn't you say? Now, the average prick is about thirteen centimetres, yes? Times three, that's thirty-nine. Times six, that's two hundred and thirty-four. Two metres thirty-four, yes?'

They were all gazing at her, most in wide-eyed amusement, some in prim disgust. 'Now, for all eighteen of us, that's a total of forty-two point one two metres a week! Imagine, forty-two metres of solid cock a week!'

There were gasps of shocked laughter and cries of outrage. One of the French girls leapt up animatedly and grabbed a stub of pencil. She seized a newspaper and began scribbling in its narrow margin. After her rapid calculations she announced gleefully, 'That means, that in the past year we've taken over two kilometres. How's that for dedicated service? They ought to give us all medals!'

'And you're proud of it,' Possy screeched, her voice quivering with her rage. 'Don't you feel absolutely disgusted? Satisfying our enemies like this? You're nothing better than—'

'Fuck off, you two-faced English cow!' Gudrun jerked herself upright, towering over Possy, her yellow hair swinging wildly. 'I heard you yelling last night while that fellow scalded both your English arses. I've heard you many a time. And it's not defiance or even agony you're screaming for. It's for pure pleasure, you stuck up little bitch!'

'Oh – I – I – oh...' Possy clamped her mouth shut. Tears stung her eyes, and she sank down scarlet-faced at the wall of opposition she felt about her. The grain of truth in the accusation stabbed in her gut. Her mind went back to Feely, and she experienced a bitter return of the choking disappointment in her chum. All this was Feely's fault, for it was her treacherous action in deserting them that had added to the torments of conscience Possy was facing. She hoped she was suffering for it, wherever she was.

'No, no, don't turn around, my dear. Keep your eye to the hole. Don't move. I don't want you to miss a thing.'

Feely crouched on the bed, which Langfeldt had dragged over to the wall. The scene in the room into which she gazed through the hidden spyhole in the wall was sickeningly familiar to her. Her heart had thumped with painful recognition as soon as she climbed out of the staff car, into the squalid lane by the back entrance to *The Candle Flame*. It was for those visitors who for whatever reason did not want anyone to know of their presence at the brothel. As was the narrow staircase which gave them access to the upper floors without passing through the lobby or the crowded lounge downstairs.

It was not the end Feely had foreseen to such a momentous day; a day of deeply mixed emotions, the day of her graduation after the weeks of arduous preparation. She could not help feeling proud when she had donned the superbly tailored uniform; the figure-hugging belted jacket, with its epaulettes and gold buttons, the stylish skirt, the sheer stockings and smart shoes. The immaculate shirt and tie had added a provocatively androgynous touch to her beauty, as did the soft cap with shiny peak, which she placed at an alluring angle on her carefully waved dark hair. She looked good, she knew; military, yet alluringly feminine, too. The captain's insignia at her sleeve and on her shoulders made her proud.

'Make the most of it, darling,' Shaun laughed. 'You won't get much chance to wear this sort of finery too often. We don't exactly advertise ourselves, which is a pity, I think, when I look at you. You look absolutely gorgeous.' And he had taken her in his arms and held her against him while he kissed her passionately.

She had dared to imagine that at long last, after all her tortuous waiting, he might become her lover. She had eyes only for him throughout the seemingly endless ceremonies of the long day. She was aware of him all the while, as she sat with her fellow graduates, listening to the speeches of the VIP's. Most of all when she stood trembling at the rostrum, and in an unsteady voice, her accent almost faultless, repeated the oath of loyalty, while in her mind she saw Possy's blazing blue eyes and heard the condemning cry of 'Traitor!' from her lips.

Shaun, she had to admit, seemed to have no difficulty with the idea of her treason towards her own country. Unlike General Langfeldt, who had taken her aside afterwards and, after his fulsome congratulations, delicately hinted at what reparations might follow should she attempt to betray her new allegiance. 'It could be very difficult for your two English chums,' he said sinisterly. 'What is your name for them? Possy and Olly, is it?'

She had gazed in wide-eyed dismay as his threat sank deep. 'I've – I've given my word,' she murmured faintly, and he nodded, with that urbane smile.

'Of course you have, my dear. And we all know an Englishman's – or lady's – word is his or her bond.' He laughed sneeringly.

After the toasts, and the excellent dinner, she had prayed that Shaun would approach and whisper in her ear of some planned rendezvous. But it was not he, but the general who approached her.

'I have a special treat for you, after such an eventful day,' he told her, and she felt the tears stinging the backs of her eyes, could scarcely trust herself to speak when the general, arm possessively about her waist, steered her over to Shaun. 'We're leaving now,' the general said, his voice heavy with sensual meaning, and Feely felt the hot rush of colour mounting, could not meet Shaun's level stare.

'Of course.' The handsome face broke into its typical smile. 'I'll see you tomorrow, Captain Keynes. Have fun.'

And this was it. The 'fun' the general had promised her. It was perhaps a salutary reminder of her real status, Feely thought bitterly. Just as Shaun turning up at that remote cottage had been. Finding her tied down and naked after being used by her unknown assailant.

And he was still unknown. Sergeant Bruckner had vigorously denied all knowledge of it. Though he had grinned broadly when she tearfully confronted him, so that she was still almost sure it was him. Yet she blushed furiously, as always, at the way her body recorded so faithfully such shocking details; the hands and the mouth that led her to shattering climax, had felt so different. Even the brutally rampant cock that had ploughed her afterwards…

Her painful reflections were dissipated, vanished at the overwhelming shock and grief flooding her now, as she watched a laughing Shaun enter the bedroom she spied upon. He was pulling a girl in after him. The discreet light caught at her golden curls, and Feely saw Possy, her robe flowing behind her, to reveal her svelte figure in flimsy brassiere and panties of shining satin, which was all she wore underneath. Even as Feely watched breathlessly, Shaun's capable hands stripped off the scraps of Possy's clothing until the blonde stood demurely naked before him, her legs clamped together, one thigh overlapping the other in a forlorn attempt at modesty, her entwined hands extended downward to hide the sandy fleece and the pouting mound it adorned.

For one horrible second Feely wondered whether Possy knew about her, for the girls were aware of these peepholes, and that their activities might be spied on at any time.

Or could it be that Shaun himself knew? But no, she dismissed the thought as too unworthy to hold onto. He could not be so cruel. As if to compensate for her ignoble idea, she told herself that he might well be feeling bitter himself at the knowledge of what she was doing in the company of the heartless Langfeldt, now crouching behind her. His plump fingers were pressing painfully into her slender neck, to make certain she did not take her gaze away from what was taking place on the other side of the wall.

But there was no need. Despite her distress, Feely could never have torn her gaze away from the unfolding scene before her. The only danger to her not witnessing every move was the tears that threatened to erupt at any second.

Shaun had sat on the bed, and playfully pulled Possy down across his knees. Feely saw the pink heels, the dainty soles of her bare feet waving in the air as she wriggled and kicked decorously. She also noted the faint stripes marking the entrancing curve of her buttocks.

'I gave her those stripes last night.' The general's warm breath tickled Feely's ear.

Soon the weals were overlaid with the spreading rosy glow brought about by the regular rise and fall of Shaun's hand as he spanked the resilient flesh beneath him. Feely experienced a sympathetic tingle in her own buttocks, comprehensively hidden by her smart clothing, for the general had not ordered her to remove anything.

Her eye riveted to the peephole, Feely watched in anguish as Shaun thrust Possy from his knee and she scrambled up, stood there, pouting prettily while she massaged her stinging globes.

Then she waited while he slowly undressed. Crouching on the bed, Feely shivered with tormented desire. The pulse in her vagina beat fiercely and she felt the swell of her crotch against the restricting silk of her knickers, which grew ever damper as Shaun revealed his splendidly masculine body. When he stood and shrugged off the underpants which were his final covering, the play of his muscles and the dimpling hollows of his taut buttocks drove her wild. Then her gaze was drawn helplessly to that magnificent erect penis, long and potent, flushed with its hunger, jutting like a bowsprit from beneath the brown bush of his pubis. It quivered as he moved, stretched himself out on his back on the bed, and summoned the obedient Possy to him. Her fair curls lowered, her mouth stretched wide in homage, and her moist lips slid over the gleaming helm, to take in as much of that mighty column as she could.

Her cheeks pouched and hollowed, and she sucked worshipfully at his spearing manhood. For an age he hardly moved, then suddenly a tremor passed through him, and gently now, he eased her head from its station between his thighs. He lifted her by the hips, and still remaining on his back, his head and shoulders raised by the pillows, he drew her onto him. Possy spread her legs and straddled him. Feely watched in fascination, saw the dark gash of Possy's vulva, the glistening tip of Shaun's prick which nuzzled it, hesitantly at first, then slowly, it slid into the narrow divide, took possession of it, centimetre by centimetre drilling its potent length into her enveloping sheath.

Almost absently, Feely was conscious of her skirt being lifted, of the silk panties being teased down at the back, over her curving behind until the cheeks were bared, the knickers stretching between her thighs, at the level of her stocking tops.

The general's podgy fingers played along the crack of her behind, then delved further to the moist fissure of her vulva, toyed with the wiry tendrils of her pubic hair before he parted the slippery tissue and let his fingers enter her clutching wetness. Two of them probed into her softly clinging vagina. The thumb stretched upward, into the exposed cleft of her buttocks, found the puckered mouth of her anus, pressed against the tight ring of muscle, and she shivered responsively. It forced a fractional entrance, and she gasped at this unexpected intrusion, both revolted and shamefully stimulated at such a novel penetration. She was surprised when the general did not undress her.

Still she could not tear her gaze away from the unfolding pageant of sexuality taking place in front of her, so that the feel of the general's stabbing prick startled her. Her knees were still close together, her thighs held by the tightly clinging silk panties. For an instant, as the slippery helm thrust against her, Feely was afraid that he was about to attempt to force it into the virginal tightness of her anus, but then it moved downwards, to the base of her divide, sought the much more frequented passage of her vulva. Even so, because of her position and her inability to open her legs further, it was hard and painful for him to enter her thus. She felt the burning force, the pressure as he drove into her from behind, felt the weight of him, folding, bearing down on her, and she grunted with pain and with effort. There was a searing flash and he was in her, driven home, pumping back and forth, and the pain and the excitement blended, fused, and she felt the approach of her orgasm.

Weirdly in tune with the writhing couple on the bed next door, she studied Possy's slim pale form. She was sitting upright, astride Shaun, her golden head tossed back, exposing the length of her slender white throat. Her cheeks were red, her eyes closed, her features screwed up in lost ecstasy. Shaun's large hands were at her hips, and then somehow, without breaking from her, he twisted, turned her over onto her back, so that all Feely could see were her waving limbs and the rippling planes and muscles of Shaun's heaving back, his clenching buttocks. They rode to their simultaneous crescendo of joy, while beyond the wall Feely sobbed bitterly as she, too, came, juddering and thrusting back against the general's driving loins in desperate need.

At last he allowed her to pull her tearstained face away from the wall.

Her head fell wearily to the coverlet, she felt him jet his come into her, and she shivered with relief. She was fully aware of the degrading spectacle she presented, in great contrast to the naked beauty of the couple she had just observed. She was still fully dressed, down to her shoes. Her skirt was bundled up over her behind, her knickers tangled between her knees. She could feel the disordered stocking tops and dark suspender straps dragging at her thighs.

When the general went to the tiny adjoining bathroom to clean himself, she quickly readjusted her clothing. She had dried her tears, restored some semblance of order to her face and hair, by the time he returned.

'Did you enjoy the show?' he beamed, and she knew that he was well aware of what she had witnessed, that he had cruelly brought her for that express purpose.

'Of course, general,' she answered quietly. 'But there's something you've forgotten. My pleasure can't be complete yet.' She turned and swiftly, neatly, reached up under her skirt and pulled down her panties once more. She stepped quickly out of them and dropped them to the floor, then moved and knelt across the bed, flicking the skirt up onto her hips as she did so.

'Of course, my dear, how right you are.' He moved in, grinning lecherously, unbuckling his leather belt as he did so.

Chapter Seventeen

Feely's head nodded, her chin dipped towards her chest, and she jerked awake, to a full awareness of the agony suffered by her aching frame, her chafed and cramped limbs. She felt the burning circlets of the rope cutting into her wrists, the unyielding hardness of the wooden chair-back pressing into her shoulders.

Her hands had been tied behind her, her ankles bound, one to each of the front legs of the homely kitchen article. Even her bottom ached with its hours of contact with the solid seat.

She thought she had cried herself out, her face tight with the copious tears she had shed. Her eyes were puffed, and she could picture just how much of a mess she must look. To her dismay, she felt the sting of tears yet again.

She thought of crying out, shrieking for help. Maybe someone would eventually hear and come to investigate, even in this benighted spot. But she knew, even as the thought occurred to her, that she would not do so, for that would merely prove that the odious Gerald Daventry had been right in his mistrust of her. It was cruelly ironic that, having once more landed on her native shores, she should be subjected to treatment harsher than any she had suffered during her captivity. Not that it had ended, she reflected bitterly, for she was just as surely a prisoner in the bleak moorland farmhouse as she had been in the land of her enemies.

The whole scheme of their secret return to Britain had been crazy. Feely had said so, numerous times, passionately pleading with Shaun to listen to her. The night landing from a U-boat on the north-east coast, the clandestine trip to the Yorkshire moors and the isolated hideout.

'I have to come back under my own steam, as myself,' Feely had pleaded. 'Can't we concoct a story of my escape? I can't assume a false identity here, there are too many risks. What if someone sees and recognises me? And my family – I want to see them. And Possy's folks, and Olly's. I have to let them know we're still alive.'

'Don't worry, we have everything in hand,' Shaun told her reassuringly. 'You've got a specific role to play. We know what we're doing.'

Against her instincts, she accepted his word, and his leadership. She kept telling herself just being on the mission with him was enough for her. Everything – her troubled conscience, the conflict raging within that told her she must get in touch with the British authorities as soon as possible and do her duty as a patriot – all went by the board in her happiness at being at Shaun's side, facing danger with him. Both happiness and a numbing despair, for still, incredibly, he had not made love to her, in spite of the dog-like devotion she had shown, her eagerness to surrender to him. He hugged and kissed her, treated her with every sign of fondness and affection. She had done all she could, short of explicitly begging him to take her, to indicate her yearning for him.

'We must keep a clear head,' he told her gently, during their last night aboard the discomfort of the submarine. 'We can't afford to let emotion cloud our thoughts. We've got to make our task the only thing that matters. When it's done...' he smiled and put a strong hand on her wrist, and her heart fluttered with the distant glimmer of hope he offered. 'You've got a vital role to play,' he went on, his voice holding her, trapping her in its intensity. 'You know what they told you at the training school. It might well be necessary for you to use your charms, your lovely body, to achieve our aims. You won't let me down, will you, Felicity?'

Appalled, she shook her head, not trusting herself to speak.

Shag for the Fatherland! The idiotic phrase rolled around in her head while she fought against the weeping fit that threatened.

One of her consistent nightmares, both sleeping and waking, was the vision of Shaun and Possy and the naked passion of their coupling. Even now, as she thought of it, lashed to the kitchen chair in the middle of that bleak upper room in the lonely farmhouse, her stomach tightened and her vulva pulsated with jealous hunger. The ropes burned again at her ankles at her instinctive movement to draw her thighs together.

She strained, thrusting her tummy muscles forward, nipped in her buttocks and squirmed miserably. The tears began rolling again.

The cruellest cut of all was Shaun's acquiescence in this latest sadistic nonsense, initiated by the beastly Daventry. Now there was a traitor if ever she had seen one! A product of the privileged class to which she belonged, Gerald Daventry, on the surface the essence of an English country gentleman, was perfectly willing to betray Britain for the Nazi cause he had espoused long before the outbreak of war. As a schoolgirl, Feely had understood little and cared less about the antics of the lunatic fringe led by Mosley and his ilk. Now she had painfully first hand evidence of their danger.

But it was not Daventry's politics that outraged her. After all, who was she to criticise, when her own notions of right and wrong were now so uncertain? She did not know herself whether she was a patriot or a traitor. All she knew was that she could never betray Shaun, whatever might befall. No, it was their accomplice's sadistic bent, and his hostility towards her as an individual, which had disgusted and now terrified her. The final despair had come two nights before, when the bulky, florid figure had voiced his suspicions and distrust of her motives.

'I know her sort,' he declared with brutal directness. 'I've been brought up with them. They haven't an honest bone in their bodies. They're all subterfuge. They'll drop their knickers and open their legs for anyone if they think it will give them an advantage. They hold nothing sacred, least of all themselves.'

She had gazed, hot-faced and speechless at the vehemence of his attack. 'Tell him... tell him, Shaun,' she squeaked eventually. 'We haven't... we've never...' her voice faded, the blush intensifying.

Gerald Daventry threw back his head and laughed. 'My God, Launcey! You mean to say you haven't shagged it yet? What's wrong? Is she poxed up from working in that brothel? You'd better get to work and give her a jolly good poke, old boy. Otherwise, you stand no chance.' Again she gasped at the crudity of his taunt, but the rotund face changed to an expression of venomous seriousness. 'I tell you straight, I don't trust the little slag one bit. She's not going to the meeting at Scarborough; the less she knows the better. Leave her to me – I'll make her tell the truth.'

And, to her utter dismay, Shaun appeared to have taken heed. When the time approached for the rendezvous with the contact at the northern seaside town, Shaun deferred to Daventry's judgement and agreed to leave her at the farmhouse.

He had stood by and watched as the hateful figure pushed her into the chair and bound her hand and foot. Only when Gerald made to gag her with a piece of cloth had Shaun interfered. 'No,' he said calmly. 'There's no one likely to hear her. Besides,' he gave a ghost of a smile and looked at her, 'it can be the first test. You won't yell, will you?'

Tears streaming, unable to speak, she had shaken her head.

It was growing dark. She shifted uncomfortably and her breasts heaved on a sob. They had left early that morning. How much longer could she endure such agony? She could feel her swollen bladder. She no longer struggled against the bonds, but kept as still as she could. Yet even so, she could not restrain herself much longer. If nobody came soon, she would have the ignominy of wetting herself to add to her woes.

She almost did anyway, with relief, when she heard the approach of a vehicle, then the sound of footsteps and a door opening. She called out, her voice hoarse and urgent. 'Is that you, Shaun? Please be quick. Untie me. I'm bursting. I have to go!'

'Oh dear, what a shame.'

The mocking tone made her shudder, as did the sight of Daventry, in his tweed jacket and plus-fours. He was alone, and smiled with malicious pleasure at the undisguised horror etched on her face.

'Shaun's been delayed,' he drooled. 'He'll have to stay the night in Scarborough. Things to do.' He chuckled sinisterly. 'Never mind, I said I'd look after you. Gives us the chance to get to know one another, eh? To have a little heart to heart.'

She felt the courage ebbing from her, like the urine that threatened to release itself from her aching bladder. She couldn't hold back the sniffling tears. 'Please, I need the toilet.' She hated the subservience in her tone, yet she emphasised it, speaking in a whisper. 'I can't wait.'

'Nonsense, you're a big girl now,' he mocked. 'All it needs is a message from the brain, to tell the appropriate muscles that it isn't convenient. These muscles here, see?' He came forward, bent over her, and laid a large hand flat upon the curve of her stomach. She felt the tender distension of her belly, his cradling touch shockingly intimate though weirdly comforting at first, until he began to push, increasing the pressure until she wriggled desperately and cried out. Then resistance gave way. She felt the gushing release and the aching relief of letting go. The warm flow spread, down the insides of her thighs, over her bottom, and turned cold even as the drops spattered with shameful volume over the sides of the seat onto the wooden floor.

The heavy smell of the urine enveloped her, and she sobbed desolately, head hanging, while the drips subsided. Cruel fingers dug into her scalp, jerked her head up by her dishevelled hair, and he stared into the tragic face. 'You filthy little slag!' he hissed, his nose almost touching hers. But he was smiling with chilling delight. 'You'll have to be punished for that.'

His fingers moved to her white blouse. Very slowly, starting at the top, he undid the buttons, tugging the front out from the tight waistband of her skirt, separating the two halves, pushing the garment well back on her shoulders to expose the thin straps of her pretty cotton vest, and beneath them, the slightly thicker straps of her brassiere. The plunging V of the cotton garment was decorated with a fine piping of blue embroidery.

'My, aren't you the sexy one!' Daventry mocked.

He moved away from her, and Feely watched him with eyes wide with fear. 'What are you doing?' she asked, her voice cracking. 'Please, you can trust me. I'd never do anything…' she stopped, her neck and face suffused with the deep blush which spread enchantingly over her pale skin, then gulped and continued, '…to hurt Shaun.'

He spun round, his face alight with malevolent glee. 'Ah-ha! Now maybe we're getting somewhere near the truth, little miss. He's immune to your well-fucked charms, is he? That's why you're such a randy little alley cat, eh? His must be one of the few cocks in the Third Reich that hasn't nestled in your hairy hole.' He nodded at the spreading dark patch that covered her belly and the front of her thighs. 'Pissing yourself for him, you might say! Well, never mind, maybe I can give you something to take your thoughts off him for a while.'

She cringed, whimpering as he came to her with a large pair of scissors in his hand. She gave a small scream at the touch of the cold blades on her skin as, very carefully, he cut through the straps at both shoulders. Then, equally delicately he peeled down the thin vest, and eased the cups of her bra off her breasts until both the articles of clothing rested in her lap.

Her treacherous nipples began to peak at once upon being bared, even though his hands felt clammy as he cupped her breasts possessively, weighing them salaciously. He flicked his thumbs over the nipples and she shivered at the tingling response to his teasing caress. He took hold of them between thumb and forefinger, rolled them until they swelled a little more, gradually increasing the pressure until he was twisting them painfully and she cried out. He pulled, pinching and stretching the pale rounds, distorting their shape and sniggering with joy at her cries.

'Oh... *ow*... please... you – you're hurting me,' she cried quietly when he released his hold, and she hunched forward, longing to hug herself, to ease the throbbing discomfort.

Suddenly he wrinkled his nose in exaggerated disgust. 'You really do stink! I think it's time you got out of those filthy things and had a dip. But just so you don't try anything, as I'm sure they taught you all kinds of nasty tricks at that spy school.' Bewilderedly, she realised that he was right. Sergeant Bruckner had given them a rigorous course of self-defence and unarmed combat, although she suspected she would never have

189

the guts to use any of the techniques they had learned. Indeed, she could scarcely recall any of them now.

When he untied her ankles she groaned as he dragged her upright, her severely cramped muscles agonising as she tried to move. Though he had released her from the chair, he had not untied her hands, which remained pinioned behind her. And further indignity followed. He produced what she saw was none other than a stout leather dog collar, which he fastened round her neck, drawing it so tight that she feared he was going to choke her. To it, he clipped a length of linked chain as a leash, and by this means he led her, hobbling like a crone in her stockinged feet, along the draughty passage to the stark bathroom.

The geyser lit with a roar when he applied the match, and a steady stream of steaming water gushed into the old tub. Once more setting his features in a grimace of disgust, he bent and groped for the side fastening of her skirt, and the garment slithered down about her ankles. The saturated cotton panties clung like a second skin to her, showing the outline of her vulva and the dark triangle of her pubic hair, so it was hardly any more embarrassing when he tugged the undergarment down off her hips and she was able to step clear of it. The stockings were wet also, and he unclipped them from her suspenders with some difficulty, fighting them down off her legs and almost tipping her over as he hauled them off her feet. He literally tore the remnants of her brassiere and vest from her shoulders, and she gingerly obeyed his peremptory nod, and stepped naked over the high side of the bath into the hot water.

All the while he kept hold of the chain, making her

feel like a tethered animal.

He did not allow her to sit, but made her stand while, heaving on the leash with one hand, he quickly and roughly soaped her down with the other, from neck to ankles with a coarse flannel, then rinsed the lather from her. Though her skin glowed pink from the heat of the water, she was soon shivering in the chill air of the unwelcoming bathroom. Stepping from the tub, a brisk rub with a rough towel warmed her, but added considerably to her deep shame.

She knew, however, that her ordeal had scarcely begun. He dragged her, still naked, down the narrow stairs, pulling her along so vigorously that her neck was cruelly chafed by the leather band.

In the kitchen he led her to the solid door, where he wrapped the end of the chain around the coat hooks screwed into the wood near the top. She was secured with the front of her body and her nose literally up against the rough surface. Her insides churned anxiously, and she prayed for her legs not to collapse beneath her. She sobbed, knowing it was hopeless, and that her terror and submission only served to inflame him, yet she clung to the forlorn belief that her very helplessness might make whatever punishment he had in mind marginally less severe.

She even tried pleading. 'Please, I beg you,' she wept. 'I swear I won't betray you – betray the cause. I swore an oath of loyalty, and I... I love Shaun. I told you, I would never do anything to harm him, or what he believes in.' In her terror she wondered if that was true, shocked at hearing herself pronounce such sentiments.

Daventry chuckled grimly. 'You won't get the chance,

slut. I'll make sure of that.'

Feely strained to glance over her shoulder as he moved ominously behind her. He pushed a handkerchief to her face and obediently she opened her mouth, spluttering as he forced the cloth in, wadding it thickly to make an effective gag. 'No doubt you'll squeal like a stuck pig at the first sign of pain. Not that there's anyone round to hear you, but your shrieking offends me.'

He produced a long thin belt of supple leather, almost black. In her lengthy stay at the *Flame* she had become something of an expert in the art of corporal punishment, and was relieved to see it was the buckle end he wrapped around his right hand. In the manner of all true sadists, he clearly understood that the anticipation was an exquisite part of the punishment, and he was in no hurry to commence. In fact, for the first time he showed some tenderness, for he moved in close and let his hands fall on her delicate shoulders, traced the hollows and curves of her back, and stroked the taut rounds of her bottom. His fingers brushed at the deep divide, and she parted her thighs fractionally, forced herself to relax her locked muscles, in the hope that his hand might stray through to the pulsing fragrance of her damp vulva, and thus be distracted, if only momentarily, from his dreaded purpose.

He chuckled as though he could read her mind, and she sagged back weakly against him. She shivered as his light fingers were replaced by the slender softness of the strap, which he let lie in her buttock cleft, in a last obscene caress. Then he abruptly stepped back away from her, and her bottom hollowed, she whimpered through the muffling cloth, her body tensed for the onslaught.

Crack!

She jerked, striking her brow and her knees painfully against the unmoving wood, but she felt nothing of this, for her whole being was taken up with the line of fire that had been lashed across her bottom. It flamed, scorched, and she writhed in anguish, the chain twisting. Her tethered hands were like claws. She reached for the livid brand, yet the lightest touch was a refinement of her agony. She could feel the flesh rising already, could picture its blazing intensity. It burned abominably, and the fact that another did not follow it was an added torture.

She felt him tearing at the bonds around her wrists. 'Put your hands up, out of the way,' he commanded harshly. Blinded by tears she obeyed, reached up, wound them convulsively about the chain, clinging to it as though to a lifeline.

Crack!

An age later, an age of quivering, molten fear, the second blow was struck. She howled, the noise a grotesque gurgling in her throat, and she threshed, dancing like a demented marionette, flinging her legs out to the side, capering, oblivious to the degradation, lost in the red haze of pain.

He waited each time, savouring to the full the frenzied writhings of her tormented body, savouring the vivid red brands he was laying across her blistered, pale flesh, the network widening as the strokes landed above and below the quivering rounds, because of the wild abandon of her movements. The gargling noise emerging from her throat was that of a tortured animal, which was what she felt reduced to. Her face mottled, shining with tears, dribbles of saliva at the corners of her mouth, from which the handkerchief's folds projected. She hung and spun, pinioned by the collar pulling at her tender neck and the rattling chain to which she clung fiercely. She was lost to everything except the pain, until at last she yielded to it and let the life drain from her quivering muscles, absorbing the searing shocks, living with that splendid blaze of pain until it became part of her, and she was shamefully thrilled by her servitude to it, her dumb acceptance of its conquering power.

Chapter Eighteen

Feely stood bent over the upholstered back of the armchair, her head resting in its cushions. Her bottom felt swollen, the weals so closely overlaid on its surface that the tight flesh must surely burst. The agony washed over her in regular waves, which shattered at his gentle touch. She whimpered and shuddered, but could not truly move, for the torment was too intense. Then came a blessed sensation of relief as he laid the wet, ice-cold flannels over the inflamed area.

'Oh, thank you,' she blubbered cravenly, every shred of defiance or resentment long since fled.

Gerald Daventry stared at the bent, broken figure, and smiled in deep satisfaction. He felt his penis throb and stir, pushing against his clothing as it pulsed in semi-erection. The swollen helm was sticky, he could feel the clinging wet touch of his underpants. He felt good. His hand flickered with a strong urge to caress the bulging tweed at his crotch. As always, it took the infliction of pain, and the sight of his sweating efforts on the pale flesh, to spark any sign of arousal. And this little cow was exceptional. No wonder Shaun was so anxious to keep her, to break her in to be his devoted slave. He could see the attraction all right. He was impressed, then deeply thrilled, with the way she had finally taken his punishment. The subtle change in her threshing body, the sudden acceptance of her fate, his scourging blows, so that at the last there was no movement other than that soft quiver of shock as she absorbed the force of his strokes, the soft grunt of acknowledgement. And it was an acknowledgement of his supremacy, and her submission to it. This was a girl with great potential.

There was still a slight tremor of aftermath in the folded frame. He studied the slim legs with keen appreciation. The thighs were quite liberally scarred with the red stripes. They were separated, about six inches apart, and she made no attempt to close them for modesty's sake, and through the base of the buttock cleft, just below the edge of the flannel, in the tapering darkness, was the hint of her soft sex. His engorged prick throbbed again and he decided he must act, though part of him gave out derisive signals at this display of what he saw as weakness. He felt a stab of both admiration and envy at Shaun's strength of will in not touching the girl. That was the true conquest. That was what would reduce this creature to his snivelling slave, would have her crawling on her belly to attend his smallest whim.

For like all her kind, she lived for that imperious little cleft between her thighs, for that moist cunt which was the essence of her being.

With a return of anger at his own imperfect flesh, Gerald reverted to his former roughness of manner as he pulled away the cloth from her red backside, and she whimpered at the fresh burst of pain. Where he had been so tender, his hands now mercilessly seized the scalded flesh, dug like talons into the wounded curves and prised them apart.

Even the rough rasp of cloth as his trousers rubbed against her was a searing ordeal. But this died away at her fresh horror when she felt a finger prodding, searching out that tiny puckered mouth buried in the narrow valley. The fingertip felt the little button of tissue, the tight ring of muscle, and ruthlessly forced an entrance against the instinctive squeeze of resistance.

Feely was so virginally tight there that even forcing his finger a little way into that convulsing passage proved difficult. There was a new throb of discomfort at its withdrawal, and Feely sobbed in shivering relief. But only for a second, because the invasion was repeated, and this time she felt him smearing a cold, greasy substance all about the tiny fissure to prepare for what she dazedly knew was to be a novel violation of her body. It was only later, when the knowledge seemed an insignificant part of the nightmare, that she discovered he had used the butter from the kitchen table to ease his efforts.

Sure enough, she felt the spongy, slippery dome of his penis nuzzle deep into this last stronghold of her modesty, felt a blaze of new fire as his fingers tore at her, literally opening this narrowest of entrances for the vile trespass. His prick gained only a fractional admittance; the tight bud seemed in no way prepared to yield to the stabbing pressure. But then, abruptly, with a stab that caused her to yelp in anguish, the ring surrendered and his driving column sank deep, and she shuddered, a wave of limp acceptance overwhelmed her, and she hung there, buffeted against the chair while he pierced her to the full.

He could hardly move even now, so tight was her

body's hold on him, but gradually the thrusting plunges became easier, he began to piston back and forth, the crushing of her crimsoned buttocks a mere background of undefined pain against his rapier thrusts. Feely sobbed desolately. Her final shame was the revolting frisson of pleasure her body sent out in response to his stabbing possession. A shame that proclaimed itself minutes later, when his hand curled round her hip, sought the pulsating sheath of her vulva at the base of her dark, wetted fleece. The fingers delved, found the slippery channel through which, hitherto, she had thought all sexual pleasure lay. Through the thin walls of membrane she could feel him thrusting, while his fingers played with that tiny hub of her unstoppable excitement, and she screamed, bucking in frenzy under him as she came with a fierce splendour outmatching any of the numberless crises her perfidious body had already known.

When Shaun returned, the following afternoon, Feely was sitting naked at Daventry's feet, while he stretched out on the sofa in the sun-dappled parlour. The leather collar was about her neck, the silver dog chain held loosely in her new master's hand. She couldn't speak, but hung her head, choked by the tears and the sob that made her breasts quiver divinely.

'I've been giving your little bitch a few lessons in obedience.' Daventry tugged her roughly round, so that she presented her livid bottom to Shaun's view.

Though it desolated her, she was not surprised at his acceptance of his colleague's brutal treatment.

He crooked a finger under her chin, lifting her face,

down which the tears were flowing steadily. 'And have you learned anything, my dear?' he asked gently. Her shoulders heaved, and she nodded sorrowfully.

They kept her naked throughout the following days, and she had to wear the dog collar constantly. She let the chain trail down between her breasts, then wound it round her waist to keep it out of the way. Somehow, she felt that the whole bizarre episode had become another kind of test, between Shaun and her, and that if she submitted silently to all the indignities, to Daventry's sadistic treatment, she would have passed. So she became their slave, literally, cleaning up after them, preparing their simple meals.

When Daventry's own domestic servant arrived, Feely was hidden away in the attic, locked in, with only a camp bed and a rough blanket to cover her.

She lay for hours, thinking, dreaming, trying to make sense of what was happening to her – of what she was allowing to happen to her, she reminded herself.

Usually, though she tried to resist when her thoughts turned as they invariably did to Shaun, her body grew heated, and she could not help touching herself, rousing herself to a fever of desire, which she would have to alleviate, ashamed though she was of her weakness.

After more than two weeks of this slavish existence she broke down. 'Can't I sleep with you?' she begged, all pretence of any dignity or pride gone.

'I don't think we should, sweetheart,' was all he said.

That night Daventry came to her and led her along the corridor to his own room, while she pleaded with him to let her alone. She knew Shaun must be listening to her pitiful cries, but he made no appearance. Daventry fastened her by the chain to the foot of his bed and once more gave her a savage whipping with the belt, overlaying the faint wounds of her first beating with the livid new stripes of fresh torment. And afterwards he used her in the same manner as before.

Shaun was perfectly aware of her suffering, so she sought him out, away from Daventry's sneering observance. 'I – don't think I can take much more,' she murmured, unable to stem yet another spill of tears.

'Do you have a choice?' Shaun asked, in tones of gentle reason that cut her as cruelly as any of Daventry's strokes.

'I – he – he beats me – and – and – he buggers me!' The shocking word erupted and her face flamed at the expression of such inexpressible shame.

'Yes, I know,' Shaun said casually. 'He tells me you love it.'

She stared at him in anguish, unable to believe he could hurt her so. 'I hate it.' She shuddered. 'I hate him.' Then her body wilted, she shook with grief, and whispered hopelessly, 'And I love you.'

Soon afterwards things changed. For Feely any change was welcome, after the endless days of servitude. The torture of being naked in front of Shaun, of being treated with such unmitigated contempt, of being abused so brutally by Gerald Daventry while Shaun looked on and did nothing, as if he cared nothing for her at all. But all the while she could not bring herself to believe that this was the case, and when he told her of the plan her heart leapt with renewed hope. She no longer cared about any danger she might face, or about any conflict of loyalty. Shaun wanted and needed her. That was enough.

'Our man is very important,' Shaun told her. 'Very close to the government, running a vital part of the aid to Russia. He's powerful – a top civil servant, an aristocrat. And like most of us, he has a weakness.

'There's a group of them, all top dogs, but he's the one we're after,' Shaun went on. 'They have a kind of club. They meet at a house in Surrey, amongst other places. We can get you in there, and then it's up to you to trap him. We'll do the rest. Can I count on you? This is your chance.' He took her in his arms and his mouth hovered, and hers lifted eagerly, opening to meet his kiss.

The plan appeared to work far quicker and far better than they could have hoped. Her hair cut short in a gamine style, and dyed a lighter brown, furnished with a new identity and name, Feely became the latest of a select band of girls, many from backgrounds as comfortable as her own, who acted as sexual partners for the influential group of men they serviced. Whores, basically, just like the girls at *The Candle Flame*, except that these girls were paid, in many subtle and expensive ways.

Sir William Rootes was tall and gangly, bald, and with a paunch that jutted from his spindly frame in a way that made Feely snigger inwardly with wicked amusement. But it didn't stop her pleasing him, or from pretending she was smitten by him. He wasn't difficult to fool, or to please, for generally a few minutes' work on his unimpressive penis and he was heaving himself on top of her to rut furiously for all of twenty seconds before he came, with a gargling moan that announced a successful termination to the coupling.

'How was that, m'dear?' he would ask, puce-faced after sliding off her.

'Wonderful,' she cooed breathlessly, with a final little shiver for effect. 'Absolutely wonderful.'

She always felt far worse afterwards, when she left the discreet mansion where these assignations took place, for Shaun insisted on being there to meet her in the car, and on her account of what had taken place. 'Nothing special,' she would say miserably.

'You've got to persuade him to meet you elsewhere,' Shaun said, having picked her up from a particularly unsatisfactory evening at the house with Rootes. 'We're setting up a flat in Raynes Park. We'll get what we want there. Use your charms, Felicity, my love. Tempt him to come out and play.'

She thought of the spyholes at the *Flame*, and shuddered at what she envisaged would happen at the love nest, the record they would make of poor Willy's sexual misdemeanours. It was hard to imagine that the affable, comic figure might hold the fate of the nation in his manicured hands. But she didn't want to think about that.

At their next meeting Rootes' eyes widened and his Adam's apple bobbed with pure delight at the spectacle Feely presented when she removed her expensively fashionable dark dress. Underneath she wore the briefest of undergarments; a tightly laced corselet in a black froth of lace, which lifted and proffered to his enraptured gaze her pale breasts, bared almost to the nipple by the outrageous little garment. Cut high at the crotch, it trailed spidery suspender straps over the whiteness of her thighs, to meet the sheer black stockings hugging her shapely legs.

She paraded before him in her high heels, making sure that, as she preened and bent and turned, he caught the splendour of her pale buttocks, a great deal of which were bared by the shockingly diminutive cut of the novel underwear.

'I say!' he exclaimed, his eyes popping. 'What's all this?' He reached out a tentative hand and touched the buttock, and faint evidence of weals, nearest to him.

She winced realistically and gave a rueful smile, massaging the cool flesh tenderly. 'I have a bit of a jealous boyfriend in tow,' she said huskily, surprised at how skilful a whore and actress she had become. 'He wants to know where I get to these nights.'

'That's a bit thick though, isn't it?' Rootes offered gallantly, eyeing the fading ridges and licking his lips.

She turned and thrust her bottom provocatively, to allow him a closer look. 'Ooh, I don't know. Sometimes a girl needs to be kept in line, don't you think? I can be a really naughty girl sometimes. Wouldn't you like to give me a good spanking, Willy?' She pouted with wicked promise, and a vein pulsed at his temple.

'Good lord,' he blurted breathlessly.

Feely turned seductively, raised one foot to the bed and unsnapped her suspenders. She carefully rolled down her stocking, eased it and her shoe off, then did the same with the other leg. 'Now, watch closely,' she purred, turned her back to him, parted her thighs and, reaching down, swiftly unhooked the three tiny fasteners under the crotch of the corselet. '*Voila*...' She bent and flipped the tail up over her bottom, exposing it in all its glory for his reverent gaze.

Seconds later she was hanging over his knees, squealing discreetly and her feet paddling as he slapped with a novice's enthusiasm at the resilient cheeks dimpling so wonderfully and glowing ever rosier at each stinging smack he delivered.

'We've got him,' she told Shaun afterwards. Her cheeks glowed with a disciple's pride, almost as rosily as those other cheeks smarting within her underwear. 'He's agreed to meet me.' She wriggled on the car seat. 'You want to see my scars of battle?'

'You get our man hooked for us,' he said, 'and I'll personally kiss them better.'

Chapter Nineteen

The trouble was, Feely told herself afterwards, that she was too good.

Driven by shame, both at her knowledge that she was betraying her country and also whoring herself at the command of her would-be lover, she perversely gave the performance of her life at the secret love-nest in Raynes Park.

'Tighter,' she urged, when Rootes was binding her ankles with silk scarves to the corners of the bed. 'I don't want to be able to move.' She cast a quick glance up at the wall, at the framed print that hung there, behind which, she suspected, the eye of the camera would be recording everything. And behind which, Shaun's eyes would be enjoying her virtuoso performance.

When she was secured, on her front, with a pile of pillows under her belly to present her flexing bottom as an even more prominent target, she said, with another defiant look towards the picture, 'Better stuff my knickers in my mouth, darling. We don't want any nosy neighbours coming to investigate. And I want you to lay it on thick enough to make me scream. I'll never speak to you again if you don't.'

Rootes was reluctant at first, and the tentative swats with the thin strands did not even leave any marks. But at least he seemed to sense he wasn't doing very well.

'You want me to lay it on a little heavier?' he asked

doubtfully, and she nodded.

Crack!

This time both her jerking movement and the muffled squawking indicated that he had obeyed her with enthusiasm. The fire rippled over her dimpling flanks, a glowing network of red stripes left their distinctive signature, and five minutes later her throbbing buttocks were covered with the angry map of his strenuous efforts. He was blowing for breath and his penis was standing with commendable rigidity.

He pulled the wet silk from her mouth like a conjurer, but when he started to untie her she panted, 'No, Willy,' and lifted her stinging behind lewdly up for him. 'Leave me like this.'

His temple pulsed again and moments later he had covered her spreadeagled frame, and despite her sore bottom, she thrust back to meet his pounding drives into her.

Later, dressed once more in her expensive clothes, she winced and smiled at Rootes, patting her rump. 'Something to remember you by,' she smiled prophetically.

'Splendid,' Shaun enthused as they drove back to the anonymous bedsit he used in Reading. 'Now you can leave it to us. We've just got to reel our fish in.'

'Remember your promise,' she said a little breathlessly. 'But first let me soak in a bath.'

She did that, lying back in far more than the regulation five inches of water, and trembling in both hope and uncertainty. She rubbed the flannel lightly over the cleft of her vulva under the soapy water, trailing it across her tender labia until she shivered once more and inhaled deeply in longing. Her nipples were achingly erect, rubbery little teats that sparked with sensation at her softest caress. She forced herself to wait, imagined him waiting too, across the hall, excitement mounting.

The grey morning looked even grimmer through the X marks of the tape over the windowpanes. She had put on her silk robe, and nothing else, and she faced Shaun with quivering expectancy. He was still fully dressed, and all at once a wave of fear and sadness engulfed her. She pulled at the sash of the robe, shrugged it from her shoulders, and let it ripple down around her feet. 'Please, Shaun,' she whispered huskily, her eyes sparkling in the gloom.

'You're an impatient little thing, aren't you?' His voice was amused, affectionate. 'Come here.' She moved closer and he caught her by the waist and pulled her down across his knee, her head almost touching the floor. She thought he was about to spank her, but he stroked the pink marks of the whipping on her fragrant skin. Then he bent and, very slowly, began imprinting a series of kisses all over the soft twin globes, covering every inch of their curving beauty, until she whimpered and moaned in ecstasy. She couldn't keep still, even though she tried. Her thighs, her buttocks, and her tummy clenched. She drove her sex against the trousered thigh beneath her and shuddered, on the verge of coming, feeling her juices oiling her pulsing sheath.

'Please, fuck me,' she begged, groaning in her imperative need. His fingers entered the divide of her bottom, explored the cleft until they came to the spongy wet tissue of her vulva. They probed between the slippery walls leading to the tunnel of her vagina. '*Ohhh…*' she moaned as he stroked her, and she gnawed at her bottom lip as she felt the inexorable slide towards the abyss of orgasm. She couldn't hold back and screamed, juddering as she came, twisting against the rough cloth of his trousers, grinding her flesh against him.

She went limp, hanging over his leg and sobbing desolately.

'You naughty little thing,' he chided. 'You didn't even wait, did you?'

The resounding slap of his open palm on her tender backside made her jump. Her haunches hollowed. The sting was as welcome as the previous kisses had been. 'Yes,' she blubbered, 'I am a naughty thing. Punish me, Shaun, like I deserve.' She wanted the purging fire of his chastisement to wipe out all the sordid impurities he had witnessed. Obligingly, he struck another ringing blow, and the red imprint of his hand flamed out on her flesh. 'Yes…' she sobbed, ecstatic at the bite of pain flowing through her. He did not hold back, slapping until she thought she could take no more. Then when he flung her off him she fell at his feet, lay there on her stomach, gazing up at him in dumb adoration. She did not even attempt to rub herself to ease the throbbing torment.

'Get up.' There was a new harshness about his tone, an air that did not allow for any qualification. She scrambled up at once, catching her breath, choking back her sobs, and stood trembling before him.

'My turn now, I think,' he said. 'Show me what you can do.' As he spoke he unbuttoned himself, lifted out his penis so that it hung from his flies, semi-erect, pulsing to life. She knelt, head bowed, and reverently reached for the thickening column. Its live warmth transferred through to her very core, and she gasped at its pulsing leap, responding to her feather-like caress. She bent closer, her breath warm, her lips moist and slightly parted, tentative, full of awe, to touch its satin smoothness. The column writhed, lifted into her soft caress, the roped veins showing, and she slid her fingers around it, moved them gently up and down, the foreskin moving with them. The beat of his arousal thrilled her and she gripped him more firmly, quickening her strokes until his penis was a vibrant, hardened lance of flesh, leaping against her rhythmic stimulation.

A hand lifted, fingers splayed out, to rest on her dyed and cropped head, and thrust it firmly down towards the rearing pole jutting up to meet her. With a fearful tremor of joy she poked out the tip of her tongue, touched the tiny slit at its head, and tasted the nectar of his fluid, kissing the delicately soft tissue of his helm. Her lips opened a little, to form a tight O, which fitted around that sensitive tip, her tongue flickering back and forth, back and forth, rapidly, as light as the strokes of fluttering eyelashes. Now both his hands lay on her head, holding her down, urging her unavoidably to his rampant cock. She ached with need; the sweet sensation of surrender as she opened her mouth wide, strained to cover that magnificent dome and take it inside her mouth until he hissed at the thrill it stirred in him.

Her lips stretched she speared herself on the beating column, taking it as far to the back of her throat as she could before she choked. Her nostrils flared and she gagged, her senses reeling. But still she didn't withdraw, wondering if she would pass out, if she would die from the wonder of his flesh filling her so completely. He held her to him, driving into her until her chest swelled, she thought indeed her lungs would burst, before he finally released her and she pulled away instinctively with a loud plop. But at once, with a moan of longing, she was back, mouth open, lapping, suckling at the treasure of his huge prick, the yeasty softness of his heavy balls.

She knew instinctively that he would not fuck her, that this was to be her act of homage to him. There was no need of the pressure from his hands, holding her to him, when he erupted into her throat. She swallowed his choking fecundity, lapped at the secondary oozing from the purple dome, licking him clean like a greedy child, while it coated her gleaming lips.

They travelled up to Yorkshire on a train that was packed to capacity, mostly with uniformed figures, their kitbags and rifles blocking every doorway, every inch of narrow corridor. The journey took hours, most of it through the blackout, the few lights only a shadowy diminution of the darkness. Shaun talked to a slim figure in air force blue, with flight sergeant's stripes on his sleeve, the wings of a pilot on his battledress breast. She sat in a daze of weariness, thinking only of how her life had become utterly dependent upon the handsome Irishman, and of how completely he had taken her over.

She had become a willing accomplice in her own subjection.

Even now, thinking of it, she felt her sex moisten

against the tight silk of her knickers, as though she was a vessel dedicated to him. A vessel he used with careless ownership, while denying her the acme of happiness that could only come with the joining of his body with hers.

'I don't need to fuck you to make you mine, do I?' he had asked her solemnly, lifting her chin and gazing deep into her soulful eyes, and she had shivered as she dumbly shook her head, for she realised it was true. That in some illogical way his possession of her was all the more emphatic by his very refusal to fuck her. After all, how many men had, men whose names and even faces she could not recall? Only Shaun, her one true love, had not taken her thus. It was a great and vital concession that he now permitted her to worship him with her mouth, to receive the benison of his bounty there, and to lap his spent might until she had greedily absorbed every last drop of his seed.

She started now as his hand fell confidently on her silk clad knee. 'Go with the flight sergeant,' he said, and she stared in round-eyed puzzlement, not following his drift at all, until he spoke again. 'Go on, I told him we do it for free for one of our gallant flying boys. Off you go.'

Steeped in blushes she rose, took the airman's hand, and left the compartment. He looked as embarrassed as she was, as they squirmed and inched their way down the corridor, through the throng of bodies, stepping over the bags, until they reached the lavatory. The door was open; there were two servicemen and their gear in the tiny cubicle.

'Sorry, mate,' the airman said abruptly. 'My wife

needs to go. We won't be long.'

'Gonna hold her hand, are you?' one of them sneered, but they eased out, dragged their gear after them.

Behind the locked door, knees touching, Feely and the stranger stared at each other sheepishly. 'I can't believe you're a tart,' he said clumsily. 'I mean, I can see you're real class. Bloody good looking and all that. But when he said you were a pro.' He shook his head.

'Well,' Feely said, smiling brightly despite her shame, 'if he said so, it must be true.' She leaned closer, pressed against him, offering up her parted lips. Her thigh moved between his, she felt the throbbing response at his crotch, and they kissed avidly, tongues entwining.

'There,' she panted, 'how's that?' She plucked at the buttons over his bulging crotch, and in seconds he was out of his battledress blouse and his trousers were down around his knees. His cock thrust out from his shirt and underpants, and she seized it, massaged it skilfully, and he moaned and clawed at her.

'Steady,' she warned gently. She let him go, unzipped her dress and, wriggling in the cramped compartment, slipped it over her head. He whistled appreciatively at the silk brassiere, the matching panties and the dainty suspender belt. She reached behind, unsnapped the bra catch and shrugged it off her breasts. She hung it on the door, with her dress, then bent and swiftly pushed down her panties, stepping high to remove them. She left her suspenders, stockings and shoes on. 'That'll do,' she murmured.

She pushed him firmly down onto the toilet seat. His cock stuck up like a lance, and she straddled him, seized the column as she lowered herself slowly, rubbed its tip in the length of her vulva before lowering herself further, and guiding it into her pulsing vagina. She jounced up and down, steadily at first, their rocking motion emphasised by the swaying of the rattling train. Then she worked faster, her up and down movement more pronounced, until soon she was riding him furiously, feeling his sword-like thrusts deep inside, ploughing her, and she savoured the discomfort with a savage triumph. A tart, was she? And Shaun had given her to this total stranger. So be it. She would be the best tart this fellow would ever know. He grunted under his breath when he ejaculated into her, clearly conscious of the troops outside the toilet. Feely remained still, her weight sinking down on him, their bellies resting together, and she glued her mouth to his, and kept it there in a long final kiss of intimate tenderness.

She shook her head when he shyly asked her name, and touched a delicate fingertip to his lips. 'You don't want to know,' she whispered. 'You'll never forget me, and I won't forget you. We'll always remember this moment. Good luck.'

They cleaned themselves and dressed quickly. Outside a chorus of bantering laughter went up, and they both blushed furiously as they made their way from the cramped scene of their snatched encounter.

Shaun left Feely at a cottage on the moors. Gerald Daventry was there, waiting and smiling smugly.

'I have to go,' Shaun told her the next morning, holding her hands and gazing steadily into her eyes. 'Now we can get to work on Rootes. I'll be back as soon as I can.' He turned to Daventry and said, 'She's all yours,' and Feely shivered at the ominous words.

As soon as he had gone Daventry said brutally, 'Right, get out of those things,' and he laughed savagely.

Without a word of descent she stripped, laying her clothes carefully over the back of a chair. When she was naked she stood with as much pride as she could muster, facing him, waiting.

'My word,' he said, eyeing her with a lewd leer. 'You're learning fast.' He gestured for her to turn, and she did so, giving him a view of her back, then facing him once more. 'Barely a mark on you.' He tutted, shaking his head. 'We'll have to remedy that, now won't we? Go up and get my razor strop. It's hanging in the bathroom.'

She went reluctantly, feeling the thinness of the stair carpet on her bare soles. She unhooked the broad leather strop, ran her thumb over its surface, and shivered as she dwelt on the prospect of it biting into her flesh. Her traitorous nipples were erect, her vagina wet with shameful excitement.

Back downstairs she handed it to him and stood silently. He nodded at the armchair and she moved obediently away from him, folded herself over its upholstered back, lowered her head to the lumpy cushion, and clenched her buttocks in tense anticipation.

Suddenly she jerked and the chair creaked, and the breath was torn from her, but she couldn't scream at the blazing splendour of the fire that consumed her. A deep, livid weal of scarlet scored across her bottom. She gasped at the wave of agony and cried, moaning at the force of it taking her over. The blows came, deliberately spaced, eating into her flesh until she was

214

sure the skin must be split into bloody furrows. She couldn't keep still. Her legs squirmed, her back arched, but she thrust herself down again, allowing the waves of pain to sweep through her, to take her over. She hung there in the centre of the firestorm, aware only of the pain, its possession of her, until the steady throbbing told her the beating was over.

But not the end of her suffering.

She feared and loathed far more what she knew was to follow, and steeled herself as she felt those hateful fingers pawing her, prising apart the scorched flesh, opening her obscenely to that battering thickness, in the second and far more degrading possession of her. It was what Shaun wanted, what he had decided for her, she knew, as she felt the last resistance of her body forced and conquered, the muscle yield to the implacable entrance of its merciless conqueror.

Chapter Twenty

The film flickered in the blacked-out basement. Blue drifts of smoke spiralled slowly in the beam from the projector.

In an upper room of the requisitioned country mansion, one of the two performers on the screen downstairs, unaware of this latest showing, bent his weary head and wept. Sir William Rootes' tears were of relief more than anything; relief that the ghastly business was drawing to a close.

'They're blackmailing me,' he told the senior intelligence officer, facing him across the desk. 'I first met the girl at Arty's place. You know, she was just one of the girls. But then I got involved. She was such a nice...' he stopped, blew his nose noisily into a large handkerchief, and shook his head. 'They want details of the convoys... the supplies we're sending... all that sort of thing.'

'You did the right thing,' the officer said diplomatically. 'Coming to us.'

Rootes raised his head, his expression one of shock. 'I may be a bloody idiot,' he stated with pathetic simplicity, 'but I'm not a ruddy traitor! As soon as they sent me that copy of the film...' he stopped, shook his head again, and lowered it into his hands.

Downstairs the more junior officers attached to the unit ogled and guffawed as the pathetic figure on the screen wielded the whip, and then mounted the writhing girl. Later he untied her, and she turned, wincing as she rolled over and lay back.

'Oh bloody hell!' All eyes turned in the direction of the exclamation. 'Stop it! Stop the film! There, let me see that shot again!'

'It's definitely her, sir,' Gordon Postlethwaite reported to his commanding officer a few minutes later, his face still pale from the shock of seeing the ghost that had returned to haunt him. His pallor was replaced by a crimson tide of shame as he explained to his senior officer just how he was so certain that the girl on the bed was Felicity Keynes.

'Is there anyone else who could confirm this?' his superior demanded.

'Well sir, apart from her family...' Gordon's voice tailed away. He shuddered inwardly at the memories he had spent the past months trying to suppress. The eventful months that had almost wrecked his military career, and done so much else besides to damage his ego. 'There's also her senior officer when we were over there, in France. She's Captain – sorry, I believe she's a major now – Clarissa Young, sir.'

A plan was already forming in the colonel's fertilely devious brain. 'Very well, say no more about this – to anyone. It stays with us, within these walls. I'll have a word with Sir William. Perhaps he can make amends for his foolishness.'

'He wants to see you again,' Shaun said. Feely was standing there, holding a tray in front of her. A garishly

217

floral pinafore was tied to her front, covering her breasts and her sex, but at the back she was naked, except for the thin string at the back of her neck, and another in the small of her back, both fastened in little bows. Her buttocks were still blotchy with the evidence of Daventry's latest beating, but all that was forgotten as she stared at Shaun. He had just returned after another lengthy absence, and she was feeling giddily overjoyed at seeing him again. Now the thought of escaping, at least temporarily, from the isolated farmhouse and the brutal regime of Gerald Daventry, buoyed her even further.

'He's proving to be extremely useful to us,' Shaun went on. 'A veritable mine of information. But we don't want him running dry, and he's beginning to dig his heels in, getting a little stubborn.' He grinned and chuckled. 'He's head over heels in love. Says he misses you, and that none of the other girls can satisfy him. So we'll just have to give him what he wants, eh, sweetheart?'

'Yes, Shaun, whatever you say.'

'That's my girl.'

'Now, don't go spoiling her,' Daventry brayed. 'You're far too soft. She's been as good as gold while you've been away. Got to keep her firmly in hand, as I've told you before.'

'Why don't you show me how, Gerald?' Shaun chuckled.

'Very well,' Gerald said, bristling a little at the veiled challenge to his authority. 'Come on then, slag,' he ordered, 'let's show him. Go and get it.'

Feely turned obediently and left the room. Upstairs

she stared at herself in the mirror. She clutched the broad strop at each end, parted her legs slightly, and passed its clammy smoothness between her thighs. Slowly, she rubbed it up and down, against her vulva, frotting gently while she shivered in arousal. She could feel her own filmy moisture adding to the dampness of the leather, but after a few seconds, she snatched it away and hurried from the bathroom.

Back downstairs her eyes never left Shaun's, nor his hers, as she bent over the back of the chair, keeping her locked knees primly together.

When the strop struck, with a loud crack, her frame shuddered and her head jerked up involuntarily as she gasped with the flaring pain, but then sank again immediately, while the livid brand came up on her pale flesh. By the sixth and final lash she was whimpering audibly, her body quivering, but she had stayed down. Her bottom blazed a fiery scarlet over most of its beautiful taut surface.

'That's my girl,' Shaun said again, his voice oddly tense.

His hands were like vices on her upper arms as he plucked her upright, and she leaned into him, shivering violently. He cradled her head to his chest while the violence of her grief tore through her and then subsided. 'That's my brave girl,' he whispered into her hair.

'Well, well, we meet again, you devious little bitch.' Clarry's hand was a blur as it drew back then smacked viciously into the side of Feely's face, sending her head flying to the right.

Feely tried instinctively to bring her hands up to

219

protect herself, and felt the cold iron of the cuffs bite into her wrists. Her arms were pinioned at the back of the hard wooden chair, which almost crashed over at the force with which Clarry had hit her. Her head swam, both from the blow and the whirlwind rapidity of the events that had overtaken her. One minute she was in bed with Rootes, and the next she was being dragged naked along the landing and into a neighbouring room where a whole host, including the apparition-like figures of Gordon Postlethwaite and Clarry Young, were waiting to descend upon her.

There seemed to be a lamentable absence of British decency and fair play about the whole business. 'Can't I have some clothing… a dressing gown, or something?' Feely asked weakly.

'I don't think that's necessary, do you?' the colonel snapped with cold brutality. 'We're all very familiar with your nakedness here, Keynes. We've seen just how well you whore for your Nazi friends. No need for false modesty. You're an excellent little harlot, as well as a traitor.'

She sat there, the angled light mercilessly pouring down on her, surrounded by a sea of shadowy faces. The colonel explained swiftly and concisely what they wanted. 'If you like, we'll inform your family of your capture. You'll be tried quickly by a military court, found guilty of treason, and under the emergency powers, shot for spying. And all within a matter of days.

'Or, alternatively, you tell us here and now everything – every single thing – that's happened to you since you defected.'

'Defected?' she squealed, her sense of outrage at the

220

memory of her captivity at the hands of the Lavalle family – the start of all her problems – overcoming her fear. And the two-faced cause of the entire sorry mess into which she had been dropped was standing before her like some bloody hero.

But the colonel waved away all her tears and heartfelt sense of injustice with an imperious gesture of dismissal. 'Give us every single name you've come into contact with, especially over here. And then you'll go back to them, whoever they are. We'll continue to feed information to you and your fellow spies, which you will pass on to your masters. We'll be watching you all the time, and you'll check in with us regularly to keep us abreast of what's happening. In other words, you'll be a double agent. It's your one chance of redeeming yourself. Take it and you might come out of this untarnished, at least as far as everyone outside this room is concerned. It's up to you.'

Everyone except the colonel and one other officer left the room. They even took off the handcuffs, gave her a woollen robe to wear, and some food and drink. She talked about *The Candle Flame*, about Langfeldt, about the training school. But she didn't mention Shaun.

'My only contact is a chap called Gerald Daventry,' she told them. 'Most of the time we stay at a farmhouse, somewhere in North Yorkshire.' She blushed. 'He keeps me there, like – like a prisoner. I have no clothes, and he beats me. You can see... I can show you.' She stood and turned, raised the gown at the back, displaying her bottom. 'See? You can still see the marks.'

'And what about the Irishman?' the colonel asked.

Feely prayed the colour in her cheeks would not

increase, she willed it away, pretended to fiddle with the gown, rearranging it, tying it more securely. She shook her head. 'I don't know any Irishman – only Daventry.' Her heart was thumping wildly. She sat again, leaned forward, aware that the front of the dressing gown billowed out a little, giving a glimpse of her breasts, and that the hem had slipped from her knee, showing a length of her pale thigh.

'Please,' she said intently, staring appealingly at the colonel, letting her big eyes fill with tears. 'I never meant to be a traitor. I wanted to get in touch. I've told you, I'm virtually a prisoner, when I'm not...' she put her face in her hands. 'I wanted to tell William Rootes, but I was scared. I had to think of Possy and Olly – I mean, Brenda Hind and Olivia Bowe-Wyndham. They said, if I didn't do exactly what I was told, they'd... they'd... do something terrible to them. Please, you must understand!'

Now it was the colonel's turn to lean forward, but the firm grip of his hand on her bare knee was more a touch of encouragement than any unseemly gesture. 'Very well,' he said. 'Then it's even more important that you do your job with extreme diligence from now on.'

Some time later an abrupt voice spoke on the telephone to the colonel. 'She was picked up by the Irishman, just as we thought.'

The colonel nodded grimly and put the receiver down without saying a word. He'd have that little madam's guts for garters when they were finished with her, and that was a promise.

Months slipped into another year, the tide of war turned, flowed the way of the allies, and talk was full of a Second Front.

Feely spent most of the time hidden away in Yorkshire, until the farm seemed every inch a prison. Gerald Daventry was a taskmaster in every sense of the word, and she began to feel that she really did belong to him, even more than to Shaun, who was absent for longer and longer stretches of time.

When he did appear it was invariably to take her off to another rendezvous, where she would play all kinds of deviant sexual games with unknown partners. But still, she took a perverse pride in performing well, and earning Shaun's praise.

'I do it only for you,' she told him one day, soon after the invasion of France had taken place.

He gazed at her seriously, and nodded. 'I know,' he acknowledged, unzipping his trousers, staring down at her head bobbing devotedly at his loins, felt the wet warmth of her exquisite mouth enfolding him, and strove to delay the moment of ultimate bliss. Had she knowingly betrayed him? The information coming through from Rootes, and all the other sources involving Felicity, had proved lamentably unreliable, as he had learned to his cost. The whole operation was now useless.

He would be recalled to Germany at any moment, he guessed. The only possible success had been the odd titbits he had tossed Felicity's way, or allowed her to overhear at the farmhouse, which he hoped had found their way back to the British intelligence, for they had been as useless as the stuff they had been feeding to him.

Probably, though, the poor bitch didn't even realise she was being duped by both sides. She was his, and he was perfectly aware of her slavish longing for him. He smiled down on her, and felt that extra surge of excitement at the thought of her submission, her blind obeisance. He would put her to the test very soon. As Daventry said, she was like one of his gun dogs, the bitches that lay slavering and fawning at his feet when he approached them, that would lick his hand even as it held the whip with which he would subdue them so brutally.

Shaun felt the crisis drawing close, stared down at that lovely head. Below it, he could see the twin peaks of her breasts, the girlishly pale nipples erect, and he clamped her savagely to him, and heard with a wry grimace of satisfaction her gargled gasp as she desperately swallowed the sperm he pumped into her mouth.

Chapter Twenty-One

'Shaun, you mustn't go back to the farm! They're waiting for us. The army – they're waiting to pick us up.' Feely felt faint, her head spinning. There, she had told him – and she didn't care! She was glad. He meant so much more to her than any misty notions of loyalty to king and country. Besides, the British had been using her for long enough. She was glad that things had come to a head like this. She was weary of being used by both sides.

She had just come from the bed of yet another civil servant, who would doubtless have been approached with evidence of his wrongdoing and blackmailed into treason. Except that it was all a double bluff. British intelligence were well aware of the assignation, had indeed used it to pass on information in turn. To warn her that the spy ring was at last to be pulled in, and that she was to be the perpetrator of their capture.

'When you're all back at the farmhouse, just make sure you hang this cloth out of the front bedroom window,' the stranger had said, handing her a small bundle of material. 'We'll move in right away. Stay upstairs as soon as you hear anything. You'll be safe, I promise.'

Well, now she'd committed her final act of betrayal. She'd told Shaun as they sat in the crowded buffet at King's Cross station, her bottom still smarting from the civil servant's boisterous play. She stared at Shaun, waiting in silence. She knew his mind was working things out – making plans. Would he kill her? She was shaken at the vagueness of her own reaction. Perhaps she had really lost all reason. She had begun to suspect as much, when she thought of how she had endured all the months of degradation and physical torture from the inhuman Daventry, and the worse pain of knowing that Shaun condoned it, for all his tenderness with her. Now, the thought of death at his hands, though it scared her, held a kind of noble inevitability about it.

'What are you going to do?' she asked at last, her voice a husky whisper.

He glanced at her, smiling tightly. 'Why did you tell me? Why didn't you just obey orders and let them catch us? You'd be a national heroine.'

Her eyes were huge, filled with tears of hurt as she gazed at him. 'You know why. I'd never betray you, Shaun. You should know that. I've never mentioned you to them. I love you.'

He nodded, his mind made up. 'Then we're going back home,' he said. 'To Berlin.'

Olly whimpered as Possy dabbed gently at the raised weals over her buttocks and the tops of her thighs. Soon she would do the same for Possy. Since the war had been going so badly, the games had been getting rougher at the *Flame*.

There was a madness, a desperation in the air; an eat-drink-and-be-merry fatalism. They had practically moved the club permanently into the cellars, now that the RAF was bombing nightly. And yet madam was as affectionate as ever, and the two English girls still got to occupy her bed regularly.

'We must all look after one another,' madam would say, holding them in her ample arms. 'There are bad times ahead.'

They tried not to think of the future, sought solace in the present, in each other's passionate bodies, as well as with the array of lovers that claimed them each night. 'We'll just have to stick it out, old girl,' Possy said, clinging to Olly in the rumbling darkness, their sweating bodies glued together. 'We'll be all right. As long as we've got each other.'

They often talked of Feely, and occasionally plucked up the courage to ask General Langfeldt if he knew anything of her. He still visited the *Flame* and often had them together, when he would whip them fiercely, their trussed bodies writhing in unison, their sobbing pleas music to his ears.

Sometimes, at the mention of Feely's name, he would smile mysteriously. Once he said, 'Your friend has gone home, my dears. She is doing sterling work for us.' And Possy felt terrible, sobbed inconsolably for hours after he left, for he had added ominously, 'She is afraid that something awful might happen to you two if she fails in her task.'

Stifling a groan, Olly raised herself, and let Possy stretch out on the bed in her place. She took over the task of soothing the enflamed weals on Possy's lovely backside with the flannels and cold water. Both girls glanced up indifferently as the door opened, and for a second they stared at the slim figure in the dark overcoat, the slacks, the felt hat pulled low over her brow. How deliciously butch, was Olly's first thought, for the slender frame was clearly female, and very attractive.

The stranger pulled off the hat, revealing a tousled mop of short, light brown hair. 'Hello, chaps,' she said, smiling a little uncertainly. 'I might have known I'd find you two naked together.'

They sat up with startled squeals, their aches and pains forgotten as they gaped as though confronted by a ghost. 'Feely!' they gasped, perfectly in tune, and the next moment all three were sobbing and kissing and clutching, falling in a heap on the bed, trying to convince themselves that this was not all part of some exotic dream.

'I'll show you I'm real,' Feely wept, grinning through her tears. She fought clear of her masculine clothing, soon aided by her chums' eager hands, until she was as naked and as eager to be embraced as they were. 'Oh goodness,' she moaned, minutes later, spreadeagled on her back as Possy's fingers buried in her open vulva, sought out the tiny button of her clitoris, stirring her with delicious caresses, while Olly's lips and flickering tongue played with her aching nipples. 'I've missed you – missed this – so much!' Feely groaned with heartfelt sincerity.

More long minutes passed, unmeasured. Feely was incapable of speech or thought, and gave herself over to the consuming sensations her lovers were creating. Her arching body and whimpering cries told them when fulfilment came, and she collapsed in a welter of new tears.

She sniffled, smiled ashamedly when at last she was able to think and speak again. 'It's been so long. You don't know how much I needed that.'

Olly stared, round-eyed. 'But surely, all this time, with that gorgeous hunk of an Irishman…'

'Shaun… Shaun has never made love to me,' she confessed sadly. 'Not once.'

'But you, and he…' Now it was Possy's turn to colour, and she lapsed into diplomatic silence, recalling all too vividly the experience of being screwed so comprehensively by his magnificent weapon.

They listened incredulously as Feely told her amazing tale, with many painful hesitations, for she told them unvarnished truth. For her, the time of lies and duplicity had gone, forever.

'I hope they caught that bastard Daventry, and all the rest,' she cursed with venom. 'But I couldn't let Shaun be captured. I – I don't care that…' her voice caught on a sob, but she ploughed gallantly on, '…that he's never made – had sex with me. It doesn't alter how I feel about him. He brought me back here, to you two. I really thought he would kill me and leave me behind. But he didn't,' she ended simply. Her trembling smile appeared through her tears. 'So you see, Possy old chum, I didn't really turn traitor. I've never helped the Jerries at all, really. Every piece of information was false.'

Possy seized her friend again and pulled the lovely tearful face to her breast. 'Never mind all that nonsense,' she said, trying to reassure her friend. 'We're back together again. That's all that matters.'

'And it can't be long now before it's all over,' Olly put in, her youthful tones both hopeful and uncertain. 'They say the Russians are at the border now. As long as our own bombs don't blow us up first, we should soon be free again.' They hugged and smiled encouragingly at one another, but inside, the notion of freedom filled each of them with strangely ambivalent emotions.

Possy and Olly were shocked to discover how completely they had adapted to their lives as brothel girls. While for Feely the prospect of life back with her own side, never to see the enemy to whom she felt she belonged in a way she could never imagine with any other man, was bleak indeed.

But the end, when it came, leapt upon them with frightening speed.

Air raids became almost constant, by day and night, and the girls lived in the cellars, their clients fewer and fewer. Feely prayed every day that Shaun would come once more, but he didn't.

Then, in the early hours one morning, madam appeared with a whole wardrobe of clothes and ordered the half dozen girls she had assembled to dress quickly.

'We're getting out,' she said tersely. 'The Reds will be here any day now. And you don't want the entire Red Army ploughing its way through you. Time for new pastures, my little whores!'

The three English girls stared at one another with sick indecision. The very act of wearing normal street clothes once more was strange in itself. But, finally, the months and months of ingrained submission won the day, and they obeyed madam's orders blindly, and those of the small band of soldiers who now took charge of them.

They left in a transport plane from a blacked-out airfield close to the city. The skyline was lit with heavy flashes that, the accompanying guard told them grimly, were not bombs but heavy guns.

Several hours later they landed in another darkened field, but they had glimpsed twinkling lights in the distance below as they banked to descend.

'That's a town,' Possy whispered. 'No blackout there. Where do you think we are?'

They climbed stiffly down the steps of the plane, to sit in a draughty hut. They were given coffee and sandwiches, while outside the plane was refuelled. 'Where are we going?' Possy dared to ask as they later re-boarded the aircraft.

'Somewhere where we'll be safe,' madam told them. 'Somewhere where all our worries will be over.'

'We've got to be ready,' Possy whispered urgently to her two companions, over the increasing roar of the engines as they taxied for take-off. A belated sense of patriotism stirred her, a novel sensation of taking some responsibility for their destiny after such a long interval.

When they landed a second time, the following day, they disembarked close to a sandy white beach, exotic palm trees, and there was an enervating, warm breeze that smelt of tropical vegetation, and made their European clothing cling damply to their weary bodies. But Possy's newly awakened feeling of individuality had little chance to flourish. At this latest stop, madam came over with a swarthy looking, unshaven man carrying a doctor's black bag.

'Bend over, girls,' she commanded crisply. 'Health regulations.' With instinctive obedience the girls turned, bent, and felt their dresses being hiked up over their hips. Next minute a sharp needle pricked their buttocks, just below the edge of their panties, above the tops of their stockings. The world tilted, swam dizzily as they were assisted to lie down, then they drifted off to a welcome oblivion.

When they finally surfaced, through an obstinately clinging cloud of unreality, their bottoms were sore and bruised from a number of similar jabs. Days had passed, and they were helplessly entrapped again, halfway across the world, and in a new life which, despite its exotic surroundings, had an uncanny resemblance to the old.

Feely squinted up at the swastika and German eagle flapping proudly against the brilliant azure of the cloudless South American sky. At the edge of the neat lawn, dissected by white edged, red earthen paths, the green wall of the jungle formed its impenetrable barrier. Holding the little community more securely than any rolled barbed wire entanglement, it maintained the boundaries of the isolated settlement. None of the inhabitants would dream of wandering further than the cluster of miserable huts that made up the native village just beyond the slight rise.

The impossibility of escape had been brought heavily home within weeks of their first arrival there – more than three years before, Feely reflected. It was her twenty-fifth birthday, the year 1948. Almost eight years since she had last seen her family and her friends, apart from her two comrades in misfortune. What was it Shaun had teasingly called them once?

'Whores de combat'. Yes, that was it.

Even after three long years and more, recollection of

him still brought that stab of pain, that clenching around her heart. It was so familiar it was almost welcome, a kind of sweet sorrow she hugged jealously to herself. She was sure he must still be alive, somewhere. Her fondest dream, and her favourite waking fantasy, too, when she could indulge in the rare luxury of some private moments alone, was of his suddenly turning up there, in the depths of the jungle stronghold, to claim her once again as his mistress, wife, slave. She didn't care. She was his, always would be, on any terms he demanded.

The outside world had ceased to be real for any of them. Not that they lacked visitors. Plenty of senior officers came to the new *Candle Flame* – General Langfeldt among them. Feely wondered if it were true that the war was still continuing, that Germany had made a startling recovery, thanks to those secret weapons about which rumours had flown thick and fast in the latter days. Pilotless planes that had destroyed half of England's cities, forced them to sue for peace, so that only America stood now as Germany's official foe, soon to beat an ignominious retreat.

'You'll soon be back in Berlin, madam,' the general would announce with unwavering arrogance, but madam always shook her head philosophically.

'No, this new world is good enough for me and my little moths, eh girls? *The Candle Flame* burns brightly enough out here.'

Privately, though, the girls speculated. Though the uniforms were as resplendent as ever, and some nights it felt just like the old times as the rooms of the modest buildings resounded with the laughter, and the sighs, of the busy girls and their clients, there was something that did not quite ring true about the gaiety. However, the three English girls did not trouble themselves for long over such uncertainties. More than ever resigned to their fate, they lived for the moment. They had learned that it must be enough for them.

One afternoon Feely watched her two chums approach. Possy's naked body was a deep brown, as was her own. Even the neat little patch at the base of their bellies was sun-tipped, the curls bleached by constant exposure to the sun. They never wore clothes – except the costumes they were required to don for the *tableaux vivants* madam still liked to stage. The English girls were still usually cast in the prominent roles of victim; the Churchill knickers had made their reappearance, their ceremonial lowering as popular as ever. There was to be a special show that evening, partly in celebration of her birthday…

Crack!

Feely flung back her head and screamed. She spun on the end of the rope, her tethered wrists strung above her, lashed to the stout wooden crossbar above the low platform. The velvet tropic night seemed all the blacker beyond the brilliance of the arc lamps, for the stage was outdoors, in the small compound.

The cheering clients sat or lounged on the wicker furniture spread below. The thin lash snaked wickedly over her bare buttocks, and its tip curled around her hip, bit viciously into the sensitive mound at the base of her belly. She capered and kicked, aware of how abandoned her movements were, the frank display of her sex it gave.

Crack!

The fire rippled and she did her marionette fling. As the pain bit into her she felt the strong stirrings of that other sweetly shameful fire, deep in her belly and her pulsing vagina. She shivered, her tanned body gleamed in the light, shone with the sweat she could feel streaming down over her flesh, just as she could feel the oily fluid secreting from the divide of her sex. She let the fire enter her, let the pain wash over her, absorbing it into her flesh, rejoicing at each new scorching flare of agony the whip brought.

She hung limply, head down, shivering when it was over, the burning steady. She found herself hoping that Possy or Olly would be allowed to attend her. She wanted the fierce joy of orgasm, hungered for it, but more importantly she wanted its bliss to be delivered by a lover. Not some anonymous nazi penis. She felt herself being untied. She had scarcely noted the wielder of the whip – what did it matter who punished her?

The stranger gathered her up, cradling her in his arms. She winced at his touch on the glowing weals. The world spun, and she heard madam's husky voice from somewhere behind her.

'…A special birthday treat for you, my pet… An old friend… He wants you for the night… Be good to him…'

The strong figure was carrying her easily through the onlookers, into a cool interior, up creaking wooden stairs to one of the best rooms, laying her down on the bed. She winced with pain, even at the contact of the silk coverlet, and knew that the lashes he had administered must stand out in vivid brands on her brown skin.

Feely roused herself. 'I'm sorry, sir. You – you laid it on a little heavily.'

'And you took it bravely, as always.'

Feely's eyes snapped open. That voice! Her heart thudded, then felt as if it had stopped, her breath driven from her. She stared disbelievingly, wondered if she had gone mad at last or died and amazingly discovered there was a heaven after all. Shaun shrugged off his clothing and, the moonlight gleaming on his naked body, knelt and parted her legs. His erect penis speared from his groin, aggressive and ready.

'I'll make love properly to you later,' he said. 'But first...' He descended, covered her, and drove home, deep into the clinging welcome of her sheath, into her loving body that had waited a lifetime to receive it.

Exciting titles available from Chimera

* * *

All **Chimera** titles are/will be available from your local bookshop or newsagent, or direct from our mail order department. Please send your order with a cheque or postal order (made payable to *Chimera Publishing Ltd*) to: **Chimera Publishing Ltd., PO Box 152, Waterlooville, Hants, PO8 9FS**. If you would prefer to pay by credit card, email us at: **chimera@fdn.co.uk** or call our **24 hour telephone/fax credit card hotline: +44 (0)23 92 783037** (Visa, Mastercard, Switch, JCB and Solo only).

To order, send: Title, author, ISBN number and price for each book ordered, your full name and address, cheque or postal order for the total amount, and include the following for postage and packing:
UK and BFPO: £1.00 for the first book, and 50p for each additional book to a maximum of £3.50.
Overseas and Eire: £2.00 for the first book, £1.00 for the second and 50p for each additional book.

*Titles £5.99. All others £4.99

For a copy of our free catalogue please write to:

Chimera Publishing Ltd
Readers' Services
PO Box 152
Waterlooville
Hants
PO8 9FS

Or visit our Website for details of all our superb titles and secure ordering
www.chimerabooks.co.uk